Modern Myths

Stories from the Bible

Michael Breen

For Katherine Kirwan,
who taught me the nobility of literature.

Meanwhile our eyes are fixed, not on the things that are seen, but on the things that are unseen; for what is seen passes away; but what is unseen is eternal.

2 Corinthians 4:18 (NEB)

Acknowledgements

Grateful acknowledgment is made to each of the following for permission to reprint previously published material:

Scriptural Quotations

All copyrighted scriptural quotations are under the general grants of usage specific to that translation, and are designated where appropriate in the text.

Specifically, scripture quotations marked (ESV) are from The ESV® Bible (The Holy Bible, English Standard Version®), copyright © 2001 by Crossway, a publishing ministry of Good News Publishers. Used by permission. All rights reserved.

Scripture quotations marked (NEB) are from the New English Bible, copyright © Cambridge University Press and Oxford University Press 1961, 1970. All rights reserved. Read more at http://www.cambridge.org/bibles/about/rights-and-permissions/#MFTZTeeDoo97xpi0.99. Additionally, the quotations composing the Psalm antiphon in "The Last Anchorite" are also from the NEB.

In a few instances translations of scripture are my own, and in other instances quotations are from translations in the public domain, such as the King James Version. I invite you to look them up.

Lyrics in "Restoration House"

SIXTEEN TONS

Words and Music by MERLE TRAVIS
Copyright © 1947 (Renewed) MERLE'S GIRLS MUSIC
All Rights Administered by WARNER-TAMERLANE PUBLISHING CORP.
All Rights Reserved
Used By Permission of ALFRED MUSIC

Personal Acknowledgements

Robert Mounce, one of the giants of modern Bible translation, gave his encouragement and criticism to stories he no doubt found unorthodox. I thank him.

A lecture at Glenstal Abbey by Colmán Ó Clabaigh OSB was the immediate inspiration for "The Last Anchorite." He graciously allowed me to allude to portions of his book chapter "Anchorites in late medieval Ireland," and gave thoughtful criticism to the story itself, although I suspect he did not much care for it.

Thanks are also in order to two readers, Robert Umlauf, PhD. and Tim Takacs, both of whom are thoughtful and cultured people.

Finally, I thank both of my wives, the late Lynne Crutcher Breen and Deborah Parsley Breen, both of whom are loving and long-suffering.

Table of Contents

An Evening at the Club. 9

The Mark of Cain 25

The Scapegoat 53

The Last Anchorite. 91

The Lake of Fire Church 111

Restoration House. 149

The Full Immersion Baptist Church. 169

CERN. 177

An Evening
at the Club

When the Most High parcelled out the nations,
when he dispersed all mankind,
he laid down the boundaries of every people
according to the number of the sons of God;
but the LORD's share was his own people.

Deuteronomy 32:8 (NEB)

The melodic sounds of glacial ice tinkling in leaded crystal tumblers were muffled by deep-pile carpet dyed the color of dried blood and elaborate silk tapestries in the hallways. Dense cigar smoke wafted through the rooms and down the corridors, its color muted by the low lighting and the rich darkness of ancient mahogany paneling. An occasional rumble of deep laughter moved through the building.

In the great entrance hall a variety of hunting trophies adorned the walls. There were splendid examples of elephant, tiger, elk, bear, and a few species not native to Earth. A very large *Tyrannosaurid* head was a centerpiece of the dinosaur trophies, as was a sixty-foot-long *Aggiosaurus*, taken with light tackle. The *Tyrannosaurid* hunter still liked to brag about the keen shot the kill required, at the regrettable cost of many servants and tracking beasts.

The living tapestries were fixed on brass rails mounted on seamless walls of marble, and depicted various scenes from the history of Earth. In one, a hoary god fights and kills a scaly dragon in the watery chaos before time. Using a lightning bolt to split the carcass lengthwise, he sets one half up to make the sky and the other half to fashion the earth.

In another an errant star wanders too close to the Sun, the tremendous pull of gravity from the rogue raising upon it a molten mountain that builds and builds to a million miles in height. The Sun strains and

10

resists until it can withstand no more, and in surrender, the mass of boiling hydrogen shatters into a billion fragments, only to coalesce into planets and moons that begin their timeless orbits around the Sun.

In a third tapestry Abram has slaughtered a heifer, a goat, a ram, a turtledove, and a pigeon. He has cut the animals down the middle, and laid the halves side by side. After chasing away the vultures that try to feed upon the carcasses, Abram falls into a deep sleep and descends into the land of the night terrors. As he sleeps a dancing smokepot and a flaming torch pass between the halves of the carcasses.

The mahogany bookshelves led down a separate hallway to an endless library. There the stacks of books moved off into the distance, where the lines they formed joined into a distant blur and moved upward, where they receded out of sight.

The library was famous throughout the cosmos for its exemplars of the great writings. Besides the first manuscript of Genesis, it contained the original J, E, and P sources, as well as the very first Masoretic copy. The originals of the Gospels were also archived in the library, and their brevity surprised many. The library assistants were also pleased to display two Guttenberg Bibles, and the original manuscript of the Apostle's letter to the Romans. But the library was not parochial: it included the first copy of the sayings of Confucius, the original *Bhagavad Gita*, and the first transcription of the preaching of Siddhartha Gautama. Besides the endless manuscripts, the library contained all manner of astrolabes, prisms, cauldrons, telescopes, globes, crystals, pyramids, and other archetypal oddities long-forgotten, even to the gods.

Perched upon Mount Saphon, the Club's facilities

11

spread out as far as the eye could see. There were stories upon stories of buildings, with quarters for servants, villas for dignitaries, meeting rooms, banquet halls, and a private dining area for the most important of divinities. At the base of the mountain were the double-deep head-waters of the river Mala, which cascaded down the cliffs out of sight and into time.

The Cosmogony Society was holding its annular meeting, an infrequent event whose occurrence was dictated by the eclipse of a sun by three perfectly-aligned moons in a very remote galaxy seen by a messenger whose sole purpose was to await the event, and inform his masters of its occurrence.

The meetings had been fairly routine; mostly administrative matters of no particular controversy. All had looked forward to the events that followed, including the grand feast in the massive banquet hall lit by thousands of torches in wrought iron stands. Innumerable delicacies were served along with countless flagons of wine. The evening's entertainment featured a troupe of belly dancers, music by an Elizabethan quintet, and Greco-Roman wrestling.

Afterward, several of the dignitaries were quietly invited into a private sitting area for billiards and conversation. Perfect ports and brandies were lavished upon the guests by mute servants dressed in black who moved silently, and nearly unseen. The laughter of the evening steadily became more raucous.

"Oh, ho ho haw hawww!" barked one. "That's rich!"

"Oh, it gets better. I never tire of telling it."

"Go on, go on!"

The great head of the speaker tilted slightly. Hadad's hair was an iridescent white, and very long.

12

Brushed back over his head, it framed a cleanly-scrubbed pink face and a closely-cropped white beard. He was dressed in a cloud-white silk suit and tie, with shoes and socks to match, and the attire shimmered and stirred as if mimicking the movement of the skies. On the small finger of his left hand was a gold signet ring; the seal itself was an imprint of a bull.

An impeccably manicured finger twirled the ice in the tumbler, and a puckish smile appeared. He shot the cuffs on his sky-blue shirt, and began.

"Right. It's the meeting of the Divine Assembly, the big one, and everybody's there; the sons of god, the heavenly hosts, the adversary, and the place is just packed. Truly glorious, if you ask me, and I'm not much given to that sort of thing. Anyway, most of you guys are out somewhere in committee meetings, and Elyon calls the meeting of the principals. *I'm* there, of course, and YHWH, the adversary, Osiris, Anna, and a few others, and we're trying to remember what we decided about apportioning the Earth. And no one can recall! It took us so blasted long just to agree to do it, and then how to do it, that we adjourned to reconvene some other aeon, but nobody writes down the agreement. Chaos!

"That's when the arguing breaks out, and the whole myth business gets thick pretty quick. It's not as easy as it might sound. Everyone has to have their say. The immensity of the technical details alone takes up so much ... I want to say time..." he chuckled, "but that's not right. Let's just say an aeon or two.

"And you know me, I'm an animist, I can't help myself, that's who I am. You name it, trees, dogs, goats, cats, humans, stones, everything has a soul, and I'm very happy with a creation along those lines."

"You mean you're a pantheist, don't you?" offered an onlooker.

"Or a panentheist?" said another.

"No, I don't, and I know the difference, thank you," Hadad retorted. "I like a nice, spirit-filled place, and why shouldn't the animals have spirits along with the humans? So I pitch a nice, lush habitat, plenty of rain, plenty of crops, a barren season, a fertile season, plenty of sacrifices ... you know, a nice cycle. I like cycles, day and night, sleep and waking, wet and dry, and so on."

"Hear, hear!" chirped one of the listeners.

"Round and round we go ...." said someone else.

"And that's when YHWH pipes up, "No!" he starts thundering, "No, no, no! This animism stuff will end in disaster."

"What do you mean, old boy? I ask."

The servants stepped forward simultaneously without prompting, and noiselessly replenished the drinks. The conversation paused as a few of the deities took cigars, and clipped and lit them.

"So YHWH says, 'you can't give everything a soul, you end up with too many gods, you get totemism, everyone and everything has to get an afterlife, and pretty soon everything is sacred, everybody is worshipping everything, the afterlife is every bit as busy and congested as life on Earth, and guess what? The gods, *us*, get lost in the shuffle. I will not allow it.'"

"Sounds like loads of fun to me, I say, who can complain about fecundity?"

"And he says, kind of snappy now, 'fecundity is fine for plants and animals, but not for souls. Besides, I can't have a proper sacrifice if the victim has a soul. We save souls, remember? We don't sacrifice them.'

"Well, I can see his point, we all enjoy a good sacrifice. The best parts of creation are the sacrifices, and things can get tricky when souls are sacrificed." Hadad picked up his cigar, paused for a moment as if recalling a pleasant memory, and took a very long draw. The ash had become impossibly long, but stayed intact. "There are few things more pleasurable than the perfume from the smoke of sacrifice," he murmured. "The smells of firstborn flesh roasting on the fire, the exquisite screaming...." His suit turned the color of mist.

He sipped his cognac, cleared his throat, and continued. "An exemplary vintage, that," he said. "But," he continued, "I am my animistic self, and YHWH has forgotten some of the details from the first time we laid out creation. You *can* have it all, and I tell him that. Let's apportion the Earth between the principals, and then there is something for everyone. I can tell I have his ear then. It worked the first time with him, he'd just forgotten.

"So YHWH agrees, but, there are interminable stipulations. YHWH becomes a genuine pain; and he calls his people stiff-necked! YHWH insists 'I will have my people, my portion is reserved to me,' an eternal stream of demands like that.

"And the more he talks the more wound up the old boy gets, he's pounding the table, and I can't tell if he's serious or he's putting on a show. 'I will be the author of creation,' he says, 'I am the Alpha and the Omega, who is and who was and who is to come.'

"Well, that sets everybody off. Lots of egos in the room, so to speak. Gods are shouting, chaps are getting mad, feelings are getting hurt, so we break for a while and come back, I don't know how long, but quite

15

a while, and end up in two camps. And the divisions are quite deep. In one, there is a primordial splitting of the creator, and in ours there is a split, but it is completely within the creator."

The indescribable Brahman spoke up. "But who cares? It is all the same thing, God in the world, God not in the world, God dismembered, God remembered, God knowing all but giving man free will so God can be surprised. It is all God, all Gods. All polarities."

"Quite," said another.

"Quite," said Hadad, "but try telling that to YHWH. The break doesn't help any. In all the mayhem he keeps pounding the tables, things are riotous, and he tells us it will be his way or there will be no creation at all. We have little choice but to agree. The fellow simply isn't given to compromise. He gets his portion, and the rest of us divide the leftovers.

"The Near Eastern Subcommittee, meanwhile, is in general agreement. We're all tired of working to keep ourselves alive. Why not create servants? Then we can set up lodgings on a mountain somewhere, and give it a good rest. Every god gets his people in his territory, and there's no problem with intermingling. Let the greatest god prevail among the others. He or she who gets the most sacrifices wins the prize.

"Now does that start some trickery or what?" Hadad smiled. "But the resulting gamesmanship is loads of fun, and we have a cosmic polity of sorts. And the people need us. They realize that they are weak, and must have a god or gods to protect them. They take care of us, we take care of them. And we get some pretty good sacrifices … but some of the rites do get pretty crazy!"

16

"Yes, the sheep come to mind," said Enki.

"Oh yes, the sheep," laughed Hadad. "Wherever do men come up with these things? Can you imagine? When things go bad, they split open a sheep and read the guts to find out why. I can picture a bunch of priests on a cold morning standing over steaming sheep guts, poking their noses in and trying to figure out why everything is so rotten for them. Hah, hah hahhhh!" Hadad threw his head back, laughing, his suit glimmering a bright blue as if laughing with him.

"Well," said Enki, "some of the men did get it right. They figured out that there is a divine council that sits in judgment of them. But honestly, where did they get the idea that the gods write everything down on sheep intestines and livers?"

"People are crazy," answered Hadad. "Now, where were we? Right, everything is up and going well on our end, but YHWH sets up his allotment as a man and a woman in an eternal garden, which he calls Eden, and they pretty much have the run of the place. He keeps them from the rest of us, and that's okay. Now in the version of the story that YHWH wrote the commandments are simple. There are two trees, the tree of life and the tree of death. YHWH tells them, 'do not eat of the tree of death.'"

"Wait a moment, that's not what the Book says. It says the tree of life and the tree of the knowledge of good and evil," a plump, cyan-blue god offered while stroking his scraggly beard.

Hadad chuckled. "A corruption of the original; it's somewhere in the library here. It's the tree of death all right, don't forget your polarities. So what do they do? Of course, they eat the forbidden fruit. I'm beginning

17

to see his point about having too many souls running around. Two seem difficult enough to manage.

"Anyway, the original version tells it just as it happened," Hadad continued. "Yahweh models the man out of clay, breathes life into him, and gives him woman. Everything is nice and pretty. And YHWH gets in a big way, benevolent fellow that he is, and decides that he will give them the gift of immortality through the tree of life, *but,* he lets them be the arbiters of their own fate by giving them a *choice,* the choice of which fruit to eat. I suppose you're right Brahman, god gives man choice so man can surprise god—and that he does. Too boring otherwise. But what dolt is going to pick death? This isn't exactly a hard test. But it does leave the door open for a bad decision, or perhaps for something *unforeseen* to intervene; with YHWH it's always hard to tell what he's up to. Things go haywire when he sends snake to help them with the simplest of choices, because YHWH's too busy or important to go himself."

"Yes, yes!," said one of deities. "The trickster snake! He is always tricking us!"

"YHWH does everything he can to stack the deck for the so-called choice they have to make, right? Take your pick: life or death. I get it, we have two brand new humans here and there's probably not much going on upstairs. He even sends snake to help out, except snake, prankster that he is, reverses the messages, tells them that if they eat the fruit of the tree of life they will die, the silly woman believes him, eats the fruit from the other tree, gives it to the man, he eats it, and everything goes to hell, so to speak."

"Why would snake do that? What is in it for snake?" another god asked.

18

"Good question, old boy," said Hadad. "Here's the problem with the corrupted version. Snake gets nothing. Well, he gets cursed, and doomed to crawl on his belly, and eat the dust. Not much of a bargain if you ask me. I could go on for quite a while, but suffice it to say that there are lots of problems with the Book, at least the adulterated version. But in the original, the way it really happened, the trickster gets immortality. That's the payoff. He eats from the tree of life. And now you know why serpents cast their skin every year, and are reborn to immortality."

The servants silently reappeared, but Hadad dismissed them with a wave of his hand.

"YHWH is furious, of course. He banishes the two from Eden, but he's so mad he's not exactly thinking about what he's doing, and sends them guess where? Out into the part of Earth apportioned to *us*! So, you see, we now have a cosmologic vector never intended, at least by any of us."

Another god spoke. "But why would YHWH send the trickster. It's almost as if he meant to…."

The room was silent. Someone let out a low whistle.

After a moment, a new voice spoke. "And, my friends, this story does not have a happy ending, at least anytime soon." Regal Anna was dressed in flowing yellow robes and white slippers. Her pendulous breasts were defined by a leather brace that crossed her bosom, and her rounded belly showed through the folds of satin. She had a hooked nose and shocking deep-set blue eyes, and her lips were stained the color of rowan berries. Her skin was a deathly white, and her long flaxen-flower hair wound about her entire torso. She had been quietly listening to Hadad.

19

"As YHWH created Eden," she said, "I stood on the mountains above the plains of Anatolia, the wind in my face and my hair flowing behind me, looking upon my apportionment. For many years I stepped upon the earth, and the flowers and herbs sprouted beneath my feet. When I reached up to heaven the rains came down. I looked upon my stars as they rose in the morning and the evening. Men brought me great sacrifices and gifts of food and drink. My women gave pleasure to men, and I made their beds comfortable to lie down upon together.

"And I came to grief, for before Eden I was the consort of YHWH, the Queen of Heaven when he was the Father of Years, before he became obsessed with his portion and abandoned me for his solitary life. He now tries to bind me to his pages on the Apocalypse.

"I looked and I saw Eden in the distance, with its lush forests and grazing animals. The great river flowed into Eden from eternity and divided into four rivers that flowed north and south, and east and west. YHWH made the fertilizing rains and the death of winter. The man and the woman tended the garden and the animals, they copulated, they ate and drank. And I saw snake, in his darkness, making his way toward them. Eden was not my portion, so I said nothing.

"It is when they are thrown out of Eden that the tale of man's woe truly begins," she continued. "The cosmos is shaken and disrupted. Adam and Eve are pitched into the curses of time and know death. They must procreate or die, for it is only through birth that they can live, and they start a race of men and women. The sons of the gods see the women of men and are

20

taken with their beauty and have them for their own, and from these unions are born the giants and the mighty heroes of old. Snake is loosed, man tramps across the face of the Earth, and no one knows what will happen."

Several maidens appeared suddenly, and Anna whispered some instructions to them. One of them, a beauty with hair of finely-spun gold, caused Hadad to cock an eyebrow. They vanished just as quickly.

Anna continued. "I tell you, YHWH claims he never intended any of this, and he sees it as horribly depraved. What was meant for eternal life is now destined for death. A plan for eternity is now trapped in time, and the corruption of man runs riot. YHWH's anger burns hotly but he desires to carry on the history of man, so he sent a great flood to destroy the creation and its depravity so there may be a new beginning."

"A blatant Gilgamesh rip-off, no less," scoffed Hadad.

"Indeed," Anna said, "but a clever way to try and start the true time of salvation history."

"Oh quite," said Hadad. "Never mind that his flood wiped out our people too."

"Noah and his descendants are true men and women, and not the bastards born of the sons of god and the daughters of men," Anna said. "It is the children of Noah who are chosen for the Kingdom to come.

"But Adam's genetic guilt follows man, and the sons and daughters of Noah fall into wickedness. Still desiring man's salvation YHWH must do something, so he gives man a covenant of laws. But the priests cried out, 'If we have laws we are undone. We must wipe the

21

dust from the mirror, not blot it with laws! Laws only breed more laws!' But they were made to stand before the cauldron that had the law inscribed upon it, their wrists exposed, and they screamed as they rolled their phthisic flesh across the white-hot lettering to become the prophets of the covenant.

"And the laws, so many, many of them. Do not boil a kidgoat in its mother's milk, do not take a mother bird and her fledglings from the same nest...."

"What? What in the world does that mean?" asked a deity sipping a cognac.

Anna smiled. "He loves riddles. He loves riddles only a little less than sacrifices; there is always a knowing twinkle in his eye when he speaks of these things. They are prohibitions against incest and commingling life and death. And YHWH demanded sacrifices, and the sacrifices became the currency between man and god; the blood from sacrifice etched channels in the stone of the altars.

"But man cannot keep the law, and so the sin that began with the wiles of the trickster became rampant. Men began to sacrifice each other and their children. Men ate men. YHWH believed that circumcision would replace human sacrifice, but the bloodlust in man runs much deeper than that, so the foreskins of men are cut in vain.

"The myth-making gets muddled, and men start asking hard questions. Why is there no evidence of the Israelites' captivity in Egypt? Where is the evidence of the march of the Israelites to the promised land, or of their conquests of the Canaanites? There was no parting of the Red Sea, King David was a small man with a small kingdom, and Jericho had no wall and no one lived there. What is this Book you call sacred? It is

22

no history book.

"The law of the covenant becomes the power of sin. Men worship unbelief, idolatry, and oppression. They wander the streets with their great phylacteries bound to their heads, and people are burned at the stake or stoned. By now, YHWH is a long way from his Eden. Men have reduced him to a thing."

"Chaos!" said Hadad.

"Oh my," said the plump god.

"What's a god to do?" asked another.

"He summons a rider upon the clouds…." started Anna.

Hadad interrupted her. His suit had turned storm-black. "Yes, so he did, with no credit here, I might add. The old boy is in a real pickle, so he must send someone to save the day."

"A *deus ex machina*, if you will," offered a deity.

"The original," Hadad said, "although some tiresome Greek might argue the point. And, I have to admit, it is quite a twist on anything we had seen up to that point. The Semites are sacrificing their sons right and left to appease the wrathful gods, the Jews are turning scapegoats out into the desert in droves and lopping off foreskins by the pound, and everything looks like it's going to come apart for good.

"But," Hadad said with emphasis, "the clever old boy contrives the ultimate sacrifice, the one to end all sacrifices, a sacrifice of a son, a scapegoat, the consummate appeasement and expiation, all rolled into one. He immolates his own son on a cross, the cross is a nice touch mind you, and voilà! Instant atonement! No more sacrifices, no more chaos, no more dancing around sheep guts. A new covenant of grace through faith, open to all."

"Well, almost," said Anna. "The atonement isn't for

23

everyone."

"Oh yes, their little club they don't talk about. He did reserve Israel for himself, and he chose a people for himself. Salvation is free for all, so they say, but you have to ask, and if you don't, well then...."

"Good god!" said Osiris.

"No pun intended, I hope," smirked Hadad. His suit shimmered sky-blue.

"Tell me, please, that this has a happy ending," said Krishna.

"That depends on who you talk to; only YHWH knows for certain, or perhaps not. The Jews say the gentiles are damned, and the Christians say the pagans are damned. They both say that there is a resurrection of the dead, which ought to be worth showing up for. Can you imagine the bodies popping up out of the cemeteries? So everyone is saying everything about everyone else."

Krishna chimed in, "and the Buddhists say nothing at all!" The room erupted in laughter, and on cue the servants moved in silently to attend to the wants of the gods.

Some began to wander out of the room, and conversations started up among the remaining guests.

"I am looking forward to this one. It's a cosmic hot mess."

"It's going to be a good one. They're placing wagers on when it will all go down."

"Count me in."

"Well then, I suppose all we must need do is wait for the New Jerusalem, and then we can start over again."

"Precisely."

"Indeed."

"Hear hear."

The Mark of Cain

Then the LORD said to Cain, 'Why are you so angry
and cast down?'

Genesis 4:6 (NEB)

Smelling the smoke of sacrifice, God's eyes popped open. He had commanded no sacrifice, and its fragrance was not known to Him. God went looking for Abel but could not find him.

In the expanse of the brilliant blue sky God saw a curl of white smoke rising toward the heavens. There He found Cain, standing in the field next to a low fire. The burnt bones of Abel smoldered.

"What have you done?" God cried out.

Hearing this, the man looked away. "He wanted blood and I gave it to Him. I thought it would please Him," he said to himself.

Cain looked at the vast field he had planted. Only pale straw and stubble from his crops remained, lying broken against the deep red of the earth. Here and there the green of weeds patched the surface.

In the distance where the field met the sky he could not tell where the earth ended and the heavens began: the two bled into a haze of flat purple space. The wind did not move, and the light of the sun was still.

"Cain!" God shouted. "I asked you, what have you done? Answer me!"

"My sacrifice of grain and straw displeased you," Cain answered. "So I sacrificed Abel to you. I observed the timeless rites. I killed him. I smeared his blood on my hands and my face and my body.

Then I burned the polluted parts, and ate the clean ones. Surely by this are you now pleased."

God kept shouting at Cain. "You killed him! I cannot believe you did this! This is evil and a murder! It is just as your mother dreamt, she saw the blood of your brother flow into your mouth, and you drank your fill of it. I told you to do no such thing!"

Now Cain was shouting too. "You complain of all my sacrifices. First you sniff at my grain offering, and now you bellow about this. You wanted blood, and I gave it to you. No one can please you!"

"Insolent whelp!" God yelled. "Your sacrifice was pathetic, a few grains of flax seed from the threshing floor while your belly swells with the best from the field."

"The very grain from the very earth my father came from. Your angel Michael brought me seeds, and taught me how to nurse them into the fruits of the field. It all came from you. That should be plenty enough!" retorted Cain.

God's face turned black as smoke. Poison was in His voice. "Bastard child! Now the blood of the earth cries out against you." Then God's voice lowered. "I loved Abel, and you have destroyed him."

God paused. "You must be punished."

"Punish me?" cried Cain. "What for? It was not a murder. I do not even know what murder is. It was a sacrifice. I had to kill him. And if it is a murder, it is you who killed him, not I!"

"What?" God erupted.

"I killed him, that is true," Cain said. "You want to punish me, so what I did must have been evil, for if it were not evil you would not punish me. But I did not know evil until you just now told me. Now you have opened my eyes, and I see evil. But you who create all things, it is you who made this evil in me. Do not good and evil come from your mouth? Do you not know all? You are the guardian of all, why did you let me kill him? You make the light and the dark, and nothing comes to pass unless you command it. You make peace and calamity. I thought that the world was made by your goodness, but I see that good is good only by your whim. If you had looked on my sacrifice with the same favor as Abel's my blood would not have urged me to atone with a new sacrifice. This is your fault!"

God was raging. "I did not make you do anything! I gave you freedom. Is not a runaway horse better than the stone that lies in the field? If I did not give you choice then you would be nothing, you would be some animal stupidly trudging upon the earth waiting for me to tell you what to do. The world is better with choice than without it. You made a choice. You chose evil."

"I did not. I tried to do good and now you say it is evil. What sort of God are you?"

God answered. "I am that I am. Now the very earth shall vomit you out, and shall bear for you naught but thorns and thistles. The rivers shall flow with dust and the animals shall spit their unborn out upon the ground. A wanderer shall you be for all time, and you shall not share in the world to come."

Cain began weeping. "This is more than I can bear! You placed this worm in my heart, and now I am punished for it. Only yesterday did you banish and curse my parents, and now you do the same to me. Is it your nature to banish? I am condemned to death. The animals will pursue me and devour me, and men shall seek me out and destroy me as vengeance for the death of Abel. I am alive, but I am dead. Death is my shadow. Help me. If you bear the whole world can you not bear my sin?"

God heard the plea of Cain and relented. "I shall place my mark upon you to protect you from the men and animals who seek vengeance for the death of Abel. As you wander through time you shall be neither man nor animal, and as you hover between death and immortality you shall bear my mark so that men shall know you are of me, and shall not harm you."

Then God said to the animals and to men, "No one shall harm Cain, and if anyone kills him My vengeance shall be a thousand times seven. Cain was ignorant that he should not slay his brother, and he did so to please Me. From this day forward to the end of days no man shall slay another lest he be slain."

God spoke to Cain. "Hear me. When I am gone carve a box from stone and after the bones of your brother have cooled, clean them and place them in the box where they shall await My return. Take the ashes of Abel and mix them with water; then spread them upon your face, your arms, your hands, and your body."

"Now, be still," God commanded. God picked up a rib from the bones of Abel, its tip glowing from the embers of the fire, and with two quick strokes marked the forehead of Cain.

Then God said, "you are Mine."

Cain's head was set ablaze, and the fire spread down through his body. Clutching his face with both hands he stumbled across the dark red field, screaming. He fell to the ground where he began tearing at himself and writhing among the vermin. Cain tried to open his eyes to see, but his thick, salty tears blinded him.

His pain became too much, and the world grew dim.

He awoke in the desert lying face down, his mouth filled with sand. Choking, he slowly raised himself on all fours while hacking the grit out of his throat. He could but see dimly. Cain did not know where he was for this land was not known to him. He could not remember if he had carved the box for the bones of Abel, but his naked body was caked with foul ash. He touched the inflamed mark on his head, traced it with his finger to see if it remained, and even still it burned with the heat of the sun.

The pale desert extended in a level plane in every direction, and the sun was frozen above him in the cloudless sky. There were no smells, and Cain heard nothing. He waited until he was strong enough to move; his thirst was so great he knew he must find water or die.

Cain began trudging through the fine grey sand. His feet sank deeply with each step, as if the earth meant to swallow him. With no paths or landmarks to guide him he did not know if he moved at all, or marched in a straight line or in circles because the desert always looked the same: the slight curve of the horizon did not change and when he turned to look behind him he saw no tracks.

A mighty wind storm came and the stinging sand hurtled with the howl of the breath of God following it. His belly clutched at him. He tried to catch the vermin to eat but the insects and snakes and rats were too quick. He saw trees and animals and men but as he moved toward them they became shimmering mirages that melted into the sand. The sandals on his feet rotted and fell off, and the fibers of the rough sackcloth he wore began to fray so that it hung lower and lower upon his body until it sloughed off and lay in a coiled heap. Cain rubbed constantly at the bristles of his beard, for his skin had drawn tightly upon his body. He looked down upon himself and saw how his sweat made serpentine rivulets in the crusted blue-grey ashes of Abel.

And the raw marks on his forehead still burned. When he looked at the sun to see if it had moved, he felt the crackle of its light rekindle the wounds, yet when he looked at the ground they burned with a heavy dullness that throbbed and blurred his vision, and pulled him toward the earth.

In the distance Cain saw a caravan crawling toward him. As it grew closer he saw turbaned men, their cloaked women carrying babies, and camels and donkeys. Cain beheld that they were real. He moved toward them to beg for food and water, but as he drew near shouts of alarm were raised and cries of "Murderer!" and "Monster!" pierced the air. The men lashed at the camels and donkeys to drive them away while shouting great oaths and curses at Cain.

In his nakedness Cain sank to his knees. His head bowed, he clasped his hands and held them up. "This is more than I can bear," he whispered. Then the darkness swirled down over his eyes.

When he awoke Cain saw a mountain, but he could not know if it was real: his eyes were clotted with tears and sand, and its image wavered in the heat of the desert day. Its color was as black as the deepest night. The base was several days' journey in width, and its massive, seamless basalt octagons tapered upward perfectly into a single narrow column that disappeared into the heavens.

As Cain crept toward the mountain on all fours,

a slit seemed to open above its base, and as he drew still nearer the slit became a gash and then a great jagged black mouth, narrow and curved upward at its ends. Cain struggled to his feet and stood among the fragments of octagons that had tumbled to the foot of the mountain. Clutching them, he then knew that what he saw was real.

Cain said, "This must be the mountain called Ekur."

Far above him the mouth of Ekur was barely visible, and the light scent of water drifted down to where he could smell it. Cain lost control of himself. His quickened breathing was reedy with the dryness of the desert, his withered bones and muscles seized and bent him over into a hump, and the marks on Cain's forehead pulsed and pulled him upward. He crept up the slope on all fours and came close to the opening when the rock gave way, and he tumbled down among the broken octagons. Cain tried again and again, and pulled himself up and thrust his head into the opening, but he could only see the depths of darkness inside. He felt a gush of the moist breath of the mountain, and his legs flailing, Cain pulled himself in and began to crawl over the rough teeth that cut and tore at him. As the blackness consumed him a wet coolness moved across his body that chilled his sweat and eased his pain. The light was now behind him, and before him lay nothing but the welter of darkness. The passage narrowed into a small round tunnel and the floor became smooth and slick from the wetness of the breath of the mountain. As his great thirst urged him on, Cain wriggled forward on his belly when the tunnel suddenly dropped, and he began to hurtle downward. He folded his arms alongside himself and after gaining great speed Cain shot head first off a cliff into the void of darkness, and plunged into a deep pool.

How long he sank Cain did not know, but he knew he had descended to the roots of the mountain and there he dwelt in the night. With Cain's larval kicking the ashes of Abel flaked away. He drank through his mouth and nose until his belly was full, and he felt the water seep back into his flesh and bones. In the darkness of the depths Cain did not need his eyes, so he closed them. Buoyant, undulating, Cain could hear the water sloshing in his guts as he lingered and his body slowly unfurled. He then knew hunger, so Cain gorged himself upon the pale, boneless fish he found in the crevices of the deep, and his muscles became full and strong again.

Cain's body ceased its burning. Using the tips of his fingers he touched his forehead lightly again and again and traced the thick scarring of the marks over and over, but he still could not know what they were. Hoping to see his face and the marks Cain found his way to the edge of the great pool, and there he climbed up the stone that was formed into stairs and knelt. Slowly, he opened his eyes and looked into the calm of the water, but in the silence of the great black cavern he saw only the whites of two bright orbs reflected in the smooth water, each with a raven black dot at the center. He blinked, and then blinked again.

Cain did not close his eyes. In the eternal stillness at the center of the mountain he heard for the first time the water lapping softly against unseen walls and smelled the cleanness of the air. Cain touched the wet rock and put his mouth to it, tasting its earthiness. Then, using a smooth stone, Cain scraped the last of the ashes of Abel from his body, and easing into the pool swam upon his back. Looking up he strained to see if there was any light in the darkness above, but he saw none.

Cain began to swim in long, slow circles, and the waters of the earth began to move with him. The two gained momentum until Cain rode upon the rotating waters, and whirling round and round with them he was drawn downward to the quiet center where he paused and looked while the waters moved around him. His father Adam appeared. Adam's hair was the shadow red of the sunbaked earth and his eyes were hollow. He spoke.

"Cain, Cain, can you see me?"

"Yes, I see you."

"Cain, listen to me. I am in Sheol, far below where you linger, I am in an abyss of graves where the living shades of kings and warriors have forgotten themselves and are locked in waters that do not move. Here I was sent by He who holds the keys to Death and Death's domain. Cain, do you hear me?"

"I do," answered Cain.

Adam's image quavered in the black waters. "Cain, here am I, and for my sin here I shall remain. Only God may raise me out of these smoldering waters and I do not believe He will for the anger of God burns to the very bottoms of Sheol. Is there no hope? Cain, is there no hope?"

Cain said nothing, for he did not know what to say. He remembered God's anger and that God condemned him to wander Earth, and he remembered that God had burned His mark of protection upon Cain's forehead.

Finally, Cain spoke. "Hope? Hope.... I do not

34

know that word."

"Cain," said Adam, "is death all that you and I have? We who are stained wander in this world of graves where shouts and rumors set the blotted souls astir and crave blood so we might again feel some hint of life in our veins. Is this the eternal fate? Can we not be saved?"

Cain did not know. In the cool of the mountain he felt the heat of confusion surge in his mind and his heart. God's words to him returned: "a wanderer for all time shall you be…." Cain retched, spitting bits of the white boneless fish into the water, and he rubbed the tingling scars on his head.

He stammered, "I do not know, I do not know…."

"Cain, you must find out, it is you who must find out," Adam said over and over as his image began to fade back into the water. "Death has us captive in His grip and we cannot pay His ransom. There must be a redemption—there must be. The wrath of God cannot burn forever. Leave this place and seek out God's forgiveness."

"Wait, wait," Cain said, "this mark, this mark on my head, what is it? Tell me!"

The image of Adam shuddered. "It is a strange mark, it is one I have not seen before," Adam said. "I do not know it. Did God place it upon you? If He did then joy and sorrow and day and night are yours."

Then Adam said, "Cain, do not forget my words, our hope is upon you, do not forget, do not forget, do not forget our hope…." And the image of Adam dissolved into the blackness of the deep, and the waters of the depths of Ekur continued to whirl around Cain.

He saw many images; images of children passing

through the fire, giants falling to the earth upon plains smothered with locusts, a snake eating its tail, men strapped to chairs in the darkness of caves with great fires burning behind them, swarms of butterflies that turned to stone and fell to the ground, men with two heads, the sun and moon in a single sphere, a man riding upon the clouds of heaven and all manner of strange signs and symbols that Cain did not know, and these images poured into Cain and became a part of him and Cain felt the chill of his heart and his mind grow into flames that warmed him and made his blood quicken.

Cain knew that the time had come for him to leave the mountain; his feet acted of their own and led him up the passages where the dimness faded into light until he came to the opening of a great cave that exhaled him onto the desert. The sun was low in the sky. Cain found shelter among the rock and for the first time in his memory he slept.

The light winds of morning carried the smells of flowers and fruits. Cain the grain-eater felt his belly twinge at the scents that were new and pleasing to him, so he strode in the sand toward the place from whence they came. The gray desert sand began to fade and gave way to the black earth that was good and fertile, and as he ventured farther lush green plants not known to Cain sprouted everywhere and formed a dense wall of life that stirred with birds and insects and strange, furred creatures that moved about the canopy with quickness and ease. Cain pushed through the barrier, moving the great leaves and branches aside and pulling his legs through the tangling vines until he came to an opening to an expanse of rich fields that shimmered in the sun as gentle winds moved through and combed the grasses. There the beasts lingered, raising and lowering their heads as they grazed, and the birds circled overhead in the calm sky.

Cain made his way to a great oasis where trees filled with fruit towered over a quiet pool of water. Flowers cascaded from the heights and their fragrance was heavy upon the air; the songs of birds were sweet to Cain's ears and he decided to sojourn there. The pool of water was clear, and on all fours Cain looked into its depths where the fishes swam and the water creatures crawled. Then Cain's eyes refocused and he looked at himself reflected in the stillness of the pool. He saw the marks God had placed upon his forehead: a horizontal and a vertical slash whose thick scarring intersected perfectly at the middle. He touched the center and felt a pulse through the fibrous skin.

"Who are you that made me so?" he said.

Cain stayed at the oasis for many days, the sun rising and setting and the moon waxing and waning in the steadiness of time. He thought he might stay there forever and languish in the comforts of the oasis with its satisfying fruits, fat fishes and ample waters, and the warmth of the fires he built and the beds of lush ferns he slept on. A peace was finally upon him, a peace that he believed came from his immersion in the waters of Ekur. But the nights soon brought a stench with them, slight at first, but growing slowly into an odor that pervaded the days and nights such that the flowers died, the fruits withered and fell from the trees, and the dead fish floated in the water. As Cain lay in a bed of dying ferns he thought of thorns and thistles and cursed his days.

"Are you vexed?" asked a voice. "You are not the first, nor shall you be the last. The Most High God brings grief to many a man and the sons of man."

Startled from his sorrows, Cain looked up, and perched upon a great serpent was an angel whose blackness swallowed the light of day. In his sturdy hand the angel held the reins for the serpent, whose great forked tongue slid with a pulsing ease in and out of its closed mouth. Its diamond eyes blinked and its muscles rolled down its length under the scales of its skin.

"Vexed?" answered Cain. "I now know that word. My life is a vexation. And who are you? You obviously are an angel but I did not know such blackness existed for such blackness I have not seen even in the bowels of Ekur, and so you must be something wicked or perhaps vexation itself. It is you whom I have smelled coming these days past. Say or do what you will, my life cannot be more miserable than what The Most High God has given me. Perhaps you would be kind and bring my days of misery to an end."

The black angel paused for a moment, then gushed with a laughter that shook Cain and the serpent. "A sharp tongue!" he spurted. "I see that we shall be great friends. Who am I? I am the dread in the nights; Samael I am called, and I walk in the depths of the dreams of men, and when they awaken from their troubled sleep, I wander to and fro among them taking note of their misery and whispering my dark words into their bitter ears. I sometimes sit at the left hand of The Most High God and at other times move about with the Sons of The Most High God. I am a prince if you will."

"So, Samael, how fortunate I am to meet you. I, a man of many sorrows, could use some princely company now. I have been alone since that moment on the great plain when The Most High God took the bone of Abel and scorched me as if I were some beast He wished to mark as His property, or some criminal branded with a mark of shame. The Most High God said He marked me to protect me, as if I were an immortal, but I ask you, what sort of protection is this He has given me? I live like some vermin with hardly a moment's peace, and day and night whirl inside me like an unending storm unleashed from below. So tell me Samael, whence came you and what would you have of me? Have you some good news, some hope of tranquility? Or have you tidings of more misery and despair?"

Samael answered. "Why my poor Cain, I am here to help you, to give you the other side of the story as it were. Every story has two sides you know, and you heard only half of it while The Most High God was ranting like a child who lost his favorite toy. Accusing you of such horrid things when all you intended was to give Him what He wanted, a simple blood sacrifice. He adores blood you know, and when you gave Him blood why He became apoplectic. There's no pleasing a god like that I say, no way to please Him at all. One moment He is sunny and the next moment He is the very storm itself. I have seen this sort of thing before, mind you, and it can turn out very badly."

"Yes, yes, so true," Cain said with relief. "Why, that is the very thing I said to Him, 'there's no pleasing you' I said. And all He would say is 'I am that I am' or some such riddle as that. All this guessing what He wants, no fool can ever win that game."

"Exactly," Samael said. "But here you are, liking it or not, here you are. But as I said, I'm here to help you. Perhaps we can sort things out, get you pointed in

39

the right direction so to speak."

"Another who thinks me a fool! ... do I seem so stupid as that, trickster?" Cain said sharply. "Have you not caused trouble enough? I may be glad for princely company as desperate as I am, but I have heard lo so many times the story of you in the garden with your winning words and the great agonies that followed. Why, it is you who caused me to be here in the first place. I would be at leisure in Eden had you not come along and caused my mother to eat of the apple."

"Certainly not!" Samael snapped. "I was nowhere near the place. Now here is a bad omen, for you men are difficult indeed, arguing first with The Most High God and blaming Him for your troubles, and now arguing with me and blaming me for your troubles. Is it your nature to blame all but yourself?"

"I can tell you that I would be better off without gods like the two of you!" Cain snapped.

"Without gods like us you would be nothing at all," Samael said casually. "What would you desire, being or not-being? Existence or none? You don't really believe that man was meant for timeless leisure in the Garden, do you?"

A dread moved through Cain; his bowels turned to clay, his body felt of lead, and his eyes were dimmed with fear and confusion. "How can this be?" he sputtered.

The great serpent eased closer and lowered its head until Samael faced Cain, their faces so close that each could feel the breath of the other upon him. The serpent's opaque eyelids slowly blinked vertically, and its long tongue quickly wrapped itself around Cain's body and held him fast. Cain could do nothing but look at Samael. As Samael spoke, Cain looked into his mouth and saw that it was the purest white.

"How can what be?" Samael breathed quietly. "Nothing can happen that is not of The Most High God. He does all things. And you, my friend, are His first."

"What?" Cain gasped. His constricted body found breath difficult and his mind was cloudy. "What do you say? The first what?"

"The first born of man and woman," Samael said. "And being the first makes you special. I remember it well, out you came first and there was Abel clutching your heel just after you, the two of you spilled out of your mother's womb onto the dark red earth, both of you squabbling and screaming, a bad omen if ever there was one, and you both rolling around in the dirt and grit, Eve gasping and shocked that there was not one but two of you."

"That is a lie! Abel was born well after me." Cain wheezed.

"A lie is it? How would you know? Abel was born after you, that is true, but you do not know when or how long after. Tell me, Cain, when you were born where was Adam, the man they call your father?" Samael continued.

"He was with my mother," Cain rasped.

"He was not," Samael answered. "He was in the East and Eve was in the West, hiding from him."

"Why would my mother hide from Adam?" Cain asked.

"Because she did not know what fruit would spring forth from her loins." Samael was hissing softly now, and Cain felt as if he were entranced. "Do you see?" Samael continued. "Adam first knew your mother, but then the most wily of creatures found her, and it too

41

embraced her and became one with her. Knowing she was with child but not knowing its father she fled lest Adam see proof of her infidelity burst from her womb."

Cain's eyes blazed and he moved to strike Samael in the mouth, but the serpent's long tongue held him fast as he struggled. Then Samael's words settled upon Cain, and he slowly turned his head to look down at the serpent. "You?" he wheezed. The serpent's eyelids moved in a casual, horizontal blink. The corners of its mouth were upturned slightly, but Cain could not tell if it was a smile.

"Eve did not return to Adam for a very long while," Samael whispered, "and she suckled the two of you, one at each breast. When she saw Adam all she could say was 'I have got me a man with the Lord,' and Adam who knew no better thought he had been blessed twice over with sons. He sang the praises of The Most High God. Which brings us back to you, the wrathful one. Did you not hear The Most High God when he raged against you? Did you not hear him call you 'bastard child' and 'insolent whelp'? Were you not listening? Do you think The Most High God was careless with His words?'"

Cain gulped the air as the serpent loosed its hold, but kept him aloft facing Samael. His anger had given way to fatigue, and he felt the earth pull at him.

"Here am I," Cain said, "a man of twists and turns hated by God and men, and beset upon by God and demon alike. I have no ground to place my feet upon for this serpent holds me fast. There is nothing above me. I can hardly breathe. I am caught in the air with no days of past to bring me comfort and no days of future to bring me hope. Such is my lot and the lot of men for all time."

"It is more clouded than you would know," Samael said. "Not even I know who your father is; only The Most High God knows, and do not expect Him to tell you anything. He will deny everything I have said to you, and call me a liar and a murderer. But know this, the seeds of corruption planted in your mother are within you, and your seed shall walk upon the earth for all time and your inclinations shall be evil.

"My only crime," Cain said, "is to have eyes that see good and evil."

"Oh?" Samael replied. "Killing Abel and then eating him. Isn't that a bit much?"

"I had to."

"Why?"

"I don't know."

"Are you certain you did not choose to do so? It could be called it a rebellion. Just like your parents."

"This I do not understand," Cain replied. "The Most High God tells me I am doomed to wander for all time because I am a murderer, yet places the life-giving mark upon me. Why would he condemn my evil and yet protect my life? Now you tell that the corruption of woman is in me and that I may be a bastard child. Well, which is it? I am either the chosen of The Most High God or my seed and I are condemned. So tell me, and tell me now."

"You are both," Samael said quietly.

"I cannot be both!" Cain yelled.

The serpent loosed its tongue and Cain crashed to the earth, his face buried in the dirt. From beneath the blackness of the folds in his great cloak Samael withdrew a perfect gold coin, smooth on both sides. It reflected the sun and the sky and the clouds above and the withered oasis below. He angled it in the light of the sun until it reflected onto Cain's face and blinded him.

"See this coin? It has two sides. Is not a coin a unity? Yet in its unity it must have two opposing sides, and those oppositions are in you Cain. You are in His image, but you are in my image too. When you see me, you see yourself. When you hear the thunder of the voice of The Most High God you hear yourself. When you smell the rot of burning flesh from war, you smell us both. And so, man of twists and turns, you are aswirl in the world of opposites, and the opposites are aswirl in you. And like the blank sides of this coin you cannot tell which from which, but an imprint must be put upon each side by me and by The Most High God. This is the way it must be. Now do you understand?"

"I do not," Cain answered.

"Cain, man is the only seeing eye of the deity. The Most High God needs you to see for him. We need you to see for us."

"To see what?"

"To see ourselves."

Samael flipped the coin to Cain, who caught it with both hands. "Our conversation must be lost to time, but its germs remain buried deeply in you and your children and their children," Samael said. The serpent began to turn away from Cain. "Now I must go," Samael said. "I have other matters to attend to."

"Wait," Cain said, "This mark upon me. What is this mark?"

"It is the great mark of the opposites," Samael responded, "and it shall rule the destinies of men until the end of time, but not in the ways men believe. The coin I gave you is a simple child's lesson to teach you the opposites of the cosmos. The mark upon you is the mark of the absolute and the all."

"Riddles, I get nothing but riddles," Cain said. "Off with you then, Master Samael. I know nothing more than when you first came."

"So shall it be for your seed Cain," Samael said. "Always puzzled because you have eyes and do not see, and ears but do not hear."

So Samael left Cain, who watched the serpent carry Samael into the distance. Realizing his nakedness, Cain wove clothing from the withered ferns and palms and covered himself. He made an umbrella to keep the sun off him, sandals for his feet, a hat for his head, and formed a small purse for the gold coin. Then Cain moved in the direction of the setting sun.

As Cain journeyed through the lands, crossing the rivers and climbing the mountains, he saw the expanse of the world. The herds of animals grazed, the birds flew in the sky, and the fishes swam in the streams. "I do not see the thorns and thistles, nor do I see the torrents of dust promised by The Most High God when He cursed me. Why is this so?" Cain thought. "Riddles and tricks, riddles and tricks. No one can see through them."

In time a woman came to Cain, and they walked together until they came to a hill that overlooked the green of the valley and the plenty of the waters and the animals. Cain lay with his woman and she bore him a son whose name was Enoch. Then Cain took many wives and they bore him many children, and as Cain's bounty grew he saw that his descendants needed a home. So Cain built an altar with a secret drawer and placed the gold coin in it. He gathered his people near the altar and told them, "Hear me now, my people. I tell you we shall build a city that is called Enoch after the name of my son, and this shall be the place where we shall live and die. Here we will work and trade and bear the fruits of ourselves. Do not lose sight of this altar, where we shall make sacrifices, and all that we do and make and say shall be bound together by a gold coin that I have placed inside it. The coin was given to me by a god."

A low murmur of approval moved through the people, and Cain began to build the City of the Initiated. The people carved great blocks of stone from the mountains and laid them square to form a massive wall around the city. For the gate to the city the men labored to hoist a finely-chiseled lintel across the threshold and crafted mighty doors from timbers felled in the forests. Soon the people felt safe from the marauders and beasts that might prey upon them and the city of Enoch began to build itself upward toward the heavens, and at its highest point lived the man called Cain, who surveyed the city of his creation from the spacious rooms that housed his family. At times in the stillness of the night Cain would touch the marks on his forehead, which had become dull and had no feeling at all.

Cain took many wives and they bore him many sons. The sons of his sons gave birth to the herdsmen and the musicians and the craftsmen, and Enoch flourished and its people spread out upon the face of the earth and founded new tribes and cities so that The Most High God and Samael both could not but hear the bustle of men at all times.

"See how Cain thrives?" Samael asked The Most High God. "What if you were to take everything from him? Would he curse you all the more?"

"Let us leave that for another time," said The Most High God.

"So be it," Samael said, "but I tell you the sons of Cain shall someday deny you and say that you do not exist. How can a God be a God if men do not say there is a God?" The Most High God said nothing.

Rivers of blood flowed from the altar as the men slaughtered the animals, and The Most High God found pleasing the scent of the smoke from the burning carcasses. And then the men began to slaughter their first born sons; the sticky blood clung to the altar and did not wash easily away, and The Most High God became accustomed to and secretly found the smell of the youthful, burning flesh pleasing.

In the evenings the men would meet at a great stone basin at the center of the city that had been hollowed out by the wind and the rain. There the light of the fire flickered orange and red on their faces. Cain's days had grown in number and it was said he was 900 years old. As he stroked the length of his flecked beard Cain spoke of The Most High God and Samael, and his voice echoed against the cut rock and blunt stone.

"I had to kill him. Abel was wholly pure and good, and purity and goodness cannot exist by themselves in this polluted world, they are bound up in men with the shadow, and men must have the shadow just as the shadow must have them. And then they are one. When I sacrificed Abel I became him and he became me, and I believed it would make me right with The Most High God. And indeed, out of Abel's death came life and men and this city."

The young men muttered, "these things we do not understand. How can good and evil be one and be the same and be not the same? How is it you became Abel and he became you?"

Without thought Cain traced the mark on his forehead, and the movement did not go unnoticed. "This I do not understand either, but I know it to be true," Cain said. "Just as I do not understand The Most High God. When He came upon the smoking bones of Abel in the field He raged and cursed me and shouted out that I was a murderer, a word I did not know, and that I had killed a man he loved. Then He cursed me."

A beardless man blurted, "Truly, The Most High God is a stiff-necked God!" The sound echoed over the silence around the basin, and an elder quickly pulled a thin piece of bone from the folds of his robe and said the words written upon it: "In the name of the god who created the heaven and the earth I exorcise every wicked and evil demon in this place!" Then, looking sharply at the young man he said, "Now be silent!"

Cain took no notice. "When I cried out for mercy He made a great oath to protect me and give me life and branded me like a slave. How is it I am marked for death and yet immortal? How is the God whose mouth speaks calamity a holy God? Men find their peace in Him and He protects some while others die of disease and war."

"Is this all there is meant to be?" an old man said softly; he kept saying it over and over in the rhythm of an ancient lament.

"No," Cain said, "there is this blackness called Samael, and how he differs from The Most High God I am not certain. At times I see the two, and at times I see but one and the same. Just as the goodness of Abel knows the shadow so does The Most High God know

48

the blackness of Samael."

In his room that night Cain knelt and breathed out a simple prayer:

"You alone are God,
  You are the first and the last,
  There is no other God besides you.
  You are the unrivaled God
  Who has no like."

In the days that followed, the ancient Cain lay splayed on the flat of his back upon his straw bed, and the fevers of dreams began to flow through him. When he awoke he remembered little but the endless urges of the unseen that were his nameless companions through the day. Then an eagle began to appear in Cain's dreams, and at first the great bird was made of rough, pitted stone with its feathers carved into neat rows and its head rotated to one side so that a single, stolid eye looked directly at Cain. The eagle came many times, always still and silent until, one by one, it began to lose its feathers, and in the place of each lost feather there appeared a small shaft of light. And with each new dream the eagle lost more feathers and its light became greater and greater until its brilliance occupied the whole of Cain's dreams so there was no room for darkness.

When Cain awoke one morning, the eagle was perched in his window with the sun rising behind it so that Cain could hardly see it. A loop of fifteen figs was around its neck. The eagle spoke: "Cain, I have been sent by The Most High God. It is His will that you know that the fullness of time has come and to prepare yourself to leave this place. He sends this gift of figs and bids you to eat of them. You will know when your time to leave has come and you will know where to go."

Cain answered with a question, "Am I going to

49

die? Is He going to kill me? For all of my days I have been haunted by life and haunted by death. I do not understand what I do. I do not understand what He does. The Most High God confounds me. He condemns me and burns me with His mark, He makes me to wander all my days while He is silent. Now The Most High God tells me to make myself ready and sends ... figs?"

The eagle said nothing.

"There it is. When men ask the hardest questions The Most High God remains silent. Very well, great bird, leave your figs. I suppose that death is all that there is."

The eagle spoke again. "Cain, touch your forehead."

Cain felt of himself and the mark was gone. He touched it again and again and the smoothness of his skin startled him.

"Cain, you have done what The Most High God sent you to do."

The eagle lifted its luminous wings and flew away. Cain looked at the figs and saw the juice flowing from them in their ripeness. He tasted one and then another until he had eaten them all. So rich was their goodness that Cain was at peace and did not fear death.

In the seven days that followed, the sun began to grow larger and brighter until there were seven days of light in one and the sun was the size of seven suns. None but Cain could see this light of the first day. He knew that it was time for him to leave Enoch, the place of his home. As he stepped through the gate of the city its great stone lintel cracked in two and crashed to the ground behind him. Cain took no notice. The great sun was low in the East and Cain began his slow walk toward it. The people of Enoch gathered in silence to watch as Cain diminished in the distance. Those with the keenest of eyes said they saw a great eagle circle down from above and fly alongside Cain until, finally, the two disappeared with a small flash.

The Scapegoat

When Abram was ninety-nine years old the LORD
appeared to Abram and said to him, "I am God Almighty;
walk before me, and be blameless, that I may make my
covenant between me and you, and may multiply you
greatly." Then Abram fell on his face. And God said to
him, "Behold, my covenant is with you, and you shall be
the father of a multitude of nations. No longer shall your
name be called Abram, but your name shall be Abraham,
for I have made you the father of a multitude of nations. I
will make you exceedingly fruitful, and I will make you into
nations, and kings shall come from you. And I will establish
my covenant between me and you and your offspring
after you throughout their generations for an everlasting
covenant, to be God to you and to your offspring after you.

Genesis 17:1-7 (ESV)

This is what the Lord GOD showed me: behold, a
basket of summer fruit. And he said, "Amos, what do you
see?" And I said, "A basket of summer fruit."

Amos 8:1-2 (ESV)

53

WE OBSERVE THE SOLEMN RITES in the manner required by the LAW. We, a miscarried people expelled from the land of our fathers countless generations ago, we who are anguished exiles in an alien land are oblivious of whether our iniquities have been confessed to the LORD GOD. We hear rumors upon rumors of troubled times, of a Messiah, of the destruction of a second Temple. The memory of my people watching Aaron place his hands upon the goat and sending it into the wilderness is as remote as this unholy land where we dwell. How may a fallen people appease the LORD GOD and remove our guilt?

The ancient, bearded men sitting at the great mountain basin we use for the meeting place tell the legend of our journey to Parthia. "May the LORD GOD have mercy on us for our sins," they say. "We became the false Israel, we turned away from the LORD GOD, our hearts were like stone. And the LORD GOD punishes us."

"No," says another, "the LORD GOD has forgotten us."

"The mighty Nebuchadnezzar," croaks a bent old man, "he came down upon us with his soldiers, swelled with pride from his victory over the Egyptians. Our fathers were like lambs ready for slaughter and that devil marched his men into Jerusalem. We could do nothing. We fought, and they burned the city and leveled the walls. He took our King and his court and sent them into the wilderness. The Temple, the LORD

GOD'S Temple, was destroyed. And we were destroyed with it. The LORD GOD rejects His covenant people, and forsakes His promises to the people of David. Jehovah-Jireh, hear the cries of your people!"

The sun edges behind the mountains and a deep shadow comes across the basin; but here time moves like a tortoise so that we cannot see the darkness come upon us. In the dim light the beards of the men become like dusky wool, bobbing as they speak.

"And then ... and then," sputters another old man, "with honeyed words Nebuchadnezzar's general told our fathers that our new king was our protector, that it was necessary to remove us from the promised land to prevent our capture by the enemies that surround us. 'Make peace with the King of Assyria' he said, 'and come to me. I swear upon the graves of my ancestors that each one of you will eat of his own vine and his own fig tree. Each one of you will drink from his own well. I will take you away to a land of safety like your own land, a land rich with grain and wine, with vineyards and olive trees and honey. You will prosper all your days, and grow fat from the fruit of the fields. You shall live, and never die.' Fools! Our fathers were all fools! But what does a defeated people do? We followed his words into the wilderness, believing that someday we would return to our tribe. Now we know the claws of a great lion shredded our people into remnants, the power of its blow scattering us across the world...."

"Yes, the land of the sun, they told us," spits the first old man. "In the East is a land filled with grain and wine, with bread for our children, and grass for our beasts. But we are the animals penned up in this land the LORD GOD has forgotten. Lies! It was all lies!

The sins of our fathers are upon us!"

They are right. My ancestors were herded into the desert like animals whose flesh is half-eaten when it comes from the womb, and forced onward to this barren land left to gnaw at the dry ground in darkness. My father's father, whom I called Abba, and who awaits the resurrection in his box of bones, tells me the stories told by his father's father, whose memory of the stories told by the oldest men of his time is sealed as tightly as his eyes.

"The caravan of our people stretched into the desert beyond seeing," Abba says. "The waves of heat were so thick that the dust and sand flowed like moving pillars of stone. The scouts looking down from the mountains said the tens of thousands of swarming people pulsed like the broken coils of a serpent, in some places a thick and dark mass, but in others a beast that dissolved into the thinness of a few staggering souls. Those at the front tried to carry the banner of our tribe but the men, burdened by the heat, little food, and no water, tottered back and forth and let the banner drop into the sand and dust. The braying animals, stumbling from thirst, kicked the desert into the air. The throng was a great, lurching viper looking for the passage to return to the world of Moloch."

Thousands of my people died, but not before they beheld the land between the rivers and saw the vastness of the walls of Babylon.

"Behold worms," said one of the guides, "the greatness of Nebuchadnezzar, your conqueror who visits divine judgment upon you. Only one who has the might of God is allowed to create such wonders. Are you still surprised that your god has forsaken

56

you and allowed the destruction of his temple?" The people were shocked by these words, but some agreed with the guide. "Only a mighty god could create such things!" they said. "Is there a God besides Jehovah?" others asked. Enraged, the elders chased them through the streets, beating them.

Babylonia was indeed a wondrous place, a great marvel that men will remember for all of time. As our ghostly parade approached the city we saw fields upon fields of crops. The trees hung heavy with fruit, olives, and nuts. Earthen jars filled with water, honey, and oil lined the streets all the way into the city.

"Is this the promised land?" some said. "Have we been misled? How can the LORD GOD bestow such abundance upon the enemy of His chosen people?" The elders rushed around, shouting, and tried to make us look at the ground as we moved through.

A horde of generous gods seemed to inhabit the city. The people spoke strange languages, and some spat at my people. The men wore rich clothing and moved with importance, followed by scores of attendants and slaves. The animals were fat with grain and water and bleated in contentment, and bare-breasted women openly suckled their children. The marketplaces were crowded and there were all manner of foods, many not known to us. Plump children bustled around great platters of seasoned meats and sweet delicacies. Strings of garlic and peppers and bundles of flowers hung from the stalls, and fruits and vegetables spilled from the tables onto the streets. Whole goats roasted on spits above careful fires, and the juices from the sizzling flesh dripped onto the flames in sputters that sounded like the busyness of the marketplace itself. We were overcome by the smells and our empty bellies grabbed at us; but we had no gold or silver and nothing to trade, so we shuffled along looking down at the stones in the street.

The great ziggurat caused even more wonder. "It reaches to the sky! It must lead to the treasure-house of the LORD GOD! That is how these people prosper! They are climbing the stairs and stealing from the LORD GOD!" said an old man. "It seemed true," Abba said. "So great was it that it looked as if the Nephilim had built it, stacking the massive and perfect stones atop each other, a labor of the centuries that only giants could perform. The straight lines of the many long stairways reached so high that they joined in the distance and went out of sight. For some it was fearful. 'Does it go to heaven? Cannot the demons rush up and conquer heaven? No, said others, this is how the angels will rush down upon men and slaughter them on the Day of the LORD GOD!'"

As our fathers passed by, they saw the squat moon faces of guards in small, boxed windows looking like the seeing eyes of a many-faced god. Atop their sallow faces were square, black felt hats, and the fletching of arrows showed above their shoulders. We could see their dark eyes follow us as we moved, but their heads stayed still. "Why would soldiers be needed to protect a god?" some asked. Others spat into the dust. "They sacrifice women and children! They are devils!" But there was a disquiet among us all, for mere men cannot build such great temples. Men cannot build such great cities. Was there more than one god? Were the holy words of fire and smoke, of the one great and powerful LORD GOD whose vibrant silence maintains us, were those holy words false?

We continued on toward the East winding upward

through the plains and barrens farther into the sky. The animals croaked and their ribs hove in the thin air, and our heads became light while with every step the earth pulled fiercely at us. As we moved during the day, the light bent and flowed around us just as the wind does, and at night the stars we had watched for generations swirled above us. Great mountains arose in the distance. They were capped in white and gleamed brilliantly in the sun. A boy cried out, "Look, the land of the gods!" and an elder who heard him dragged him away and beat him severely.

By now what meager provisions we had when we left Jerusalem were gone, and we could not slaughter any of our herd for fear that our bellies would overcome us and we would have nothing when we reached our destination. The guides left to go hunting and came back with all manner of strange animals we had never seen. "The land here is plentiful," they said. Some of the animals had smooth skin, others fur. Our hunger seized us, and we quickly skinned and roasted them. Only after our bellies were full did anyone ask what we had eaten. "Why do you want to know, fools?" replied a guide. "We caught beautiful hares and fat lizards and you ate like a king. Now you ask what you have been fed?" Women fainted and men wretched behind rocks. "We are unclean!" the people cried. A man ran among us clutching his head, yelling "I cannot vomit, I cannot vomit!" An old man wailed, "Jehovah-M'Kaddesh! Have mercy upon us and take no offense from the sin of a people who have been tricked!"

"And so was the slow undoing of our people," Abba said, "for as we travelled across the vastness of a forsaken land we suffered the thousand eruptions of a diseased remnant that died as it walked."

At camp on an open plain one night, men on horseback suddenly appeared, as if brought forth by the night. Our guards had not heard them. "Peace," one of the horsemen said in a broken Greek. "I am told that you journey to Parthia. That is the land of our fathers."

"Yes, yes, peace to you," said a startled guide. "We are here at the bidding of the mighty Nebuchadnezzar, whose might and greatness as a god and king is known throughout the world and for all time. We are guaranteed by him safe passage for these happy Jews to the lands of your fathers. We have a writing with us with his mighty seal proving this, should you like to see it."

"That is not necessary, we know of your great king. We are men of no army nor are we watchmen, you need not fear us. We are mere nomads who ride the wind about this land," said their leader.

"Jews, eh?" a rider said in his wretched Greek. "I have never seen a Jew before. Do you eat your children as I have heard, Jew? Or do you pass them through the fire?" As the guide translated the insults for the others, one of our men started to his feet, but a guide clubbed him, and he slumped to the ground as the guide shouted, "Sit, vermin!"

"A thousand apologies for the insolence of these Jewish dogs," he said. "Now, what do you call yourselves, wanderers?"
"It is good you stopped that man, we would not have been so kind. We are the Aryaka," the leader replied.

Another guide spoke up, "Ah, the men of the moon god from the fabled Ellasar. I know your language! Come Arians and make camp with us, and

60

tell us the tales of your people."

The horsemen dismounted noiselessly and tended their animals. The guides drove us away, leaving us to our grains and roots while they slaughtered one of our goats and roasted it in the fire. A few of us managed to get close to the feast, hoping to listen to the men talk. The guides presented the cooked head to the Arians, who told them, "your king honors us, and we give thanks to him." Then one of them raised his arms and sang a chant to their gods, and they began to eat.

The Arians wore small turbans and wrapped their faces in black cloth that wound around so that only their eyes and their sharp, long noses showed. Their robes were also black and made of a smooth hide beneath which we saw the occasional glint of long swords. Although we thought we were concealed by rock and darkness one of the horsemen kept looking directly at us; even through the shadows cast about him by the fire we could see the blackness of his eyes piercing the night.

"We are the men of Medes," started their leader. "We are friendly to the King Astyages but change comes with the man Cyrus, who would be ruler of all. I tell you, some day he will march into Babylonia, and the breath of his warriors will hang heavily upon the land of Anatolia. Many will die. Perhaps that will be a good thing for these Jews you bring. They are not welcome, and defile our land." The man snorted deeply and spat into the dust. "The sooner you move this herd of swine along the better."

We looked at each other and snickered. Gentiles calling God's chosen people unclean! I looked back and saw the one Aryan still looking at us. This time his eyes were hateful and his brows deeply furrowed.

"Perhaps," replied our chief guide, "we are but humble servants of our King and do as he commands. But enough of kings and wars. Tell us of the customs of your people."

"Our fathers taught us that we do not know time, it is a deception in the chaos of this world. If we die so what the matter? We live in our children just as our ancestors dwell in us. So we ride, following the winds among the canyons and upon the plains. Some of us ride chariots to defeat our enemies; some of us, like myself and these men, prefer to be among ourselves riding upon the darkness and the wind, killing our enemies as we find them. Our women follow us and make camp and nurse the screaming babies."

One of the guides started to pour some precious honey upon flatbread to offer to the riders, but the leader grabbed his wrist and stopped him. "Do not defile the dead!" he shouted, standing up with his hand on his sword. It alarmed us all. The guide stammered, "a thousand, thousand pardons, brother! We do not know your ways."

The guide released his arm, saying, "Peace, friend, I do not mean to frighten you. The golden honey is sacred to our dead. We serve it only to our fathers who have passed before us to honor them, and to sweeten any misery they may have." After the alarm died down the guides continued asking questions: "Friends, who are your gods?"

"We are greater than our gods; we conjure them to do our bidding. And if we can conjure them to do what we wish, then it is the power of the conjurer that we must believe in, not the gods."

"Then you are powerful men to be feared!" said a guide.

The leader said nothing and continued. "In the days before men, our fathers spoke to the gods and from them we learned power, and we learned the power of pleasing the gods. And this wisdom we have learned is itself powerful, so we master ourselves and our gods."

"I should like to have this power for myself!" said a guide.

"You are unfit for it, for it is given only to the men who have the blood of my race. If you were to hear me utter a single word of it I would have to pour molten lead in your ears, fool." In the darkness we could feel the guide shudder and see him turn pale. We sniggered that he believed in the nonsense of an unclean nomad who wandered about a desolate wasteland. As if he heard us the leader slowly turned his head and looked at us; fearful, we turned away.

"The language of the gods has become the hymns of my people and it is a treasure we hand to no one but those borne of our fathers. And through those hymns we move the sun and the moon and conquer our enemies ... but my people, now they begin to look too far inside themselves, and someday...." He stopped before he finished his words.

As he was talking one of his men got up and began dancing in a circle around the fire. Then he shifted on to one leg and with his body facing the fire extended his arm and pointed at the flames as he made small hops all the way around until he began whirling and chanting in a very low humming sound, "*Urummm, uruuummm, thummmimmm, thuuuummmimmm,*" and threw some small sticks and grains in the fire, which jumped at him. He shrieked with delight. "Hah!" he said.

Their leader smiled. "Tomorrow will be a very

good day for us. We will kill many of our enemy. He has told the gods to come alongside us, and they have heard him and agreed. So, friend, our songs are where we store our treasure," he continued, "for there we have our truth and power."

He casually reached for the roasted testicles of the goat and mashed them in the palm of his hand with his fist. Each of the men in his group then took some and ate it. Retching in silence I again looked away.

"Brother," a guide said, "I do not know that custom. Why do you do it?"

"It gives us the power of the animal, and we will use that power to defeat our enemies," he replied.

"And I, brother, rejoice that I am not your enemy, for I fear that you would eat mine!" said the guide. The leader said nothing, but his look caused me to think that perhaps this custom was not unknown to him. "So brother, if you do not kneel before your gods, is there anyone before whom you prostrate yourself?" asked a guide.

"After we burn the bodies of our dead to release their spirits we pray to them because they are our keepers. Sometimes, if we are very fortunate, we find their souls in an animal we come across. And I am very fortunate, for I found mine and have it with me!"

He produced a small cobra from the folds of his clothing, and held it up in the firelight. Our guides jumped back in alarm, and one of them ran away screaming at the top of his lungs. "There is evil magic here, there is evil magic here, we shall all die! Aieeeee!" Unmoved, the leader ran his right hand affectionately over the serpent, which had coiled up in the palm of his left hand. He then placed the beast back inside his clothing.

The fire began to fade so we crept back to our camp and wrapped ourselves in hides to keep out the cold. When we awoke the next morning the riders were gone. We looked but could not find any tracks in the sand from their horses or their footsteps.

"Demons, I knew it!" said one of the elders. "They are the horsemen of death!" shouted others.

We resumed our climb upward and came to a great plateau of rock flat in its perfection that spread out beyond what the eye could see. There were no landmarks except an occasional pile of stones that marked an altar, or covered the bones of a dead man. A few tried to start a revolt and return to Jerusalem, but the guides quickly lined them up and forced them to their knees: their necks extended, the largest of our captors stepped forward and lopped their heads off cleanly with his great sword. The blood spurted from the stubbed necks onto the pure rock, and as it spread out it formed a dark mirror in which we saw the shades of our selves. A terror seized us, for as we looked away we could not see where our bodies cast shadows, and a great wailing began among the women, followed quickly by the crying of children.

"Learn from this, vermin!" shouted the leader of the guides. He bent down and smeared the blood of our tribe upon his face. "The mighty Nebuchadnezzar is not to be trifled with! You are a conquered people, you are as nothing. His majesty Nebuchadnezzar tries to protect you from your enemies by moving you to a place of safety, and you defy him. We should slaughter you all at this very moment for you are worth less than the wretched beasts of burden you drag along with you." With these words the guides began running among us, beating everyone with their staffs. We scattered, screaming and shouting, but in this strange land we did not know where to run. Eventually, they exhausted themselves and fell hard asleep on the rock.

"I do not know when," Abba says, "but our people reached the boundary of the plateau which formed a straight edge that extended beyond sight in either direction. The people paused all along its brink and looked upon the vastness of the territory below. 'This is your new land of safety,' we were told, 'behold Khorasaan, a land of great beauty where you and your families will prosper under the blessings of the mighty Nebuchadnezzar.' Ancient rains had carved ruts deeply into the land. The rocks, blasted by the sun and the wind, peeled and flaked into leprous patches that lay about the ground, and the earthen faces of the cliffs were the color of old blood. The sand on the slopes was a powder so fine that even the LORD GOD could not shape anything into which HE could breathe life. Someone kicked a loose rock, and at the end of the day we could still hear it tumbling down the slope.

"The LORD GOD does not see us, the LORD GOD has forsaken the land, you will see still greater abominations that they commit," whispered an elder.

"It is the Valley of the son of Hinnom!" cried another elder.

"This is Sheol!" said one man.

"Fool!" said another. "Can you not feel your flesh and bones? We are not shadows. We may be living corpses, but we are still men."

"It looks as if a giant has scraped his great hands across the earth in a fit of rage," said a small boy.

The wind blew fiercely, and the sand swarmed and bit at us like small insects as it swept up from the valley below, and an unseen hand swept us all at once over the edge, and we began our long descent down the slope that emptied us at the bottom of this terrible valley. The animals, their eyes bulging and nostrils flared from terror, hurtled straight downhill on their knees, too choked from the sand, the dust, and the dryness to bellow out. The men, women, and children shouted, tumbled and slid in an endless descent toward the base and spilled out like the welter spoken over by the LORD GOD.

Many died during the journey here; their deaths were a blessing to them from the LORD GOD for the remnant of HIS people in this wasted land could count their bones. The children cowered in their mothers' skirts, unsteady on their shriveled feet and crying into their wrinkled hands. The animals, now living carcasses from little food and water, began to paw at the sand and rock and drank the rancid water that arose in brown pools from their scratching.

"The great Nebuchadnezzar has decreed that here you shall be safe from your enemies," announced a guide. "And here you shall remain until we return to restore you to the land of your beloved fathers."

They left us in a land where even the LORD GOD would not know to look. This could not be the land where the Sun rises; in this land we shall weep up and down. A great despair came upon us. Our kidneys became like stone and the heaviness that pulled them toward the earth felt as if unseen demons were clutching at our very guts.

"Surely the LORD GOD cannot mean for His chosen people to thrive in a land such as this," we said among ourselves.

But our people are a stiff-necked people, and we determined to survive. We crawled upon the land and learned its ways, and in so doing found many tunnels in the cliffs connected together like trails left by great worms burrowing in the earth. There we found shelter and streams deep in the bellies of the mountains and knew that from here the waters arose to cover the ground in the days before men. We learned to hunt animals that were not unclean and grow a spare grain upon the most barren of rock.

The craftsmen among us set out to carve a city from the naked stone of the cliffs, and as the facades of buildings began to emerge, we praised the workers and wept when we realized them to be duplicates of Jerusalem. The lines were chiseled straight and the columns rose up toward the heavens; the arches were like the eyebrows of the LORD GOD in their perfection, and at one end the clever masons built a Pool of Israel that had running water diverted from inside the mountain. Through these false entrances we scurried in and out of the homes we made in the tunnels and the caves.

In this arid land the months turned into years, which became centuries. Infrequent news came from those who spend their lives wandering upon the earth: mighty kingdoms arose and fell, new gods made themselves known while others died, a strange people with slits for eyes and skin the color of old brass moved across the world from the east. The moon and the sun circled overhead in countless turns but we knew no seasons, and the beards of the old men grew long and they died. Our brides gave their fresh fruits to their husbands and the blood of our circumcised sons spilled upon the stone floors.

But there was no word of the fate of those who prevail with the LORD GOD in the promised land. In

68

our isolation our hope, once spun like fine gold, was now as earthen pots in shards. The sole copy of the Torah we were permitted to bring turned brittle and broke into a thousand golden pieces swept away into the sun by the wind.

"The LORD GOD has forgotten us!" some said.

"No," said others, "our faithlessness and violence toward the LAW is punished. We must repent so that the LORD GOD will hear our cries. We must suffer, and pray, and be good to one another."

"How do we know that the High Priest in Jerusalem confesses our sins against the LORD GOD on the Day of Atonement?" asked an elder. "If he does not then we are an unclean people in an unclean land."

We grew silent, for no one had considered this. Our livers became as rocks, and we clutched at ourselves. A slow wail began among some, while others tore at their clothing.

Abba's father's father spoke. "Surely the LORD GOD cannot hold us responsible for the LAW when HIS people are in such dire circumstances!"

An elder replied solemnly, "No man may disregard the LAW. Israel has sinned, and each of us has sinned. Once a Jew, always a Jew. Just as the mark upon the face of Cain so does sin leave its stain upon us. As it is written, the look on their faces gives them away. Our sin, our iniquities, our wickedness must all be confessed."

Sitting deep in the cave at the basin that had become our meeting place, the elders determined that we were indeed a forgotten people and that we knew not whether our sins and the sins of the people of Israel against the LORD GOD were confessed on the Day of Atonement. "It is clear that we are not remembered, that no one confesses our guilt for us. The *satana* Nebuchadnezzar has destroyed our people and the LORD GOD has scattered the people of the tribes upon the wind like chaff. We are surely a dead people in HIS eyes; we must make the sacrifices required for the Day of Atonement ourselves and beg that the LORD GOD will hear our cries for mercy."

A man interrupted, "But the LAW, we do not know what the LAW requires. Our Torah has become like the desert where we live!"

"It is upon our lips and in our hearts," said one of the old men. "We shall perform the rites to perfection and send our sins out into the wilderness upon the goat. It is written, 'the soul that sinneth, it shall die.'"

We began the preparations, for we reckoned that the tenth day of the seventh month was not far off. We chose a high priest in the manner required by law, who called for the public fast.

"No man or woman or child may taste anything. So too shall not the flocks and the herds graze or drink of the water to quench their thirst. Every person and every thing shall be covered with sackcloth, and all shall cry out mightily to the LORD GOD. Turn back from your evil ways! Who knows but that the LORD GOD may relent and restore us as HIS covenant people. May HE turn back from HIS wrath so we do not perish."

We had but two bullocks, one a magnificent beast that somehow thrived in the poverty of our condition and the other a sickly animal that staggered about the land as if addled.

"Which shall we choose to sacrifice?" the elders asked. Some wanted to choose the lame beast and keep the best bull for breeding, but a haggard old man spoke up the loudest, saying, "we shall offer the LORD GOD our first and best fruits, and so we shall slaughter the strongest as a sign of our weakness." The other animals, a ram and two goats, were selected from the remnants of our wretched herd, and we placed them all in separate pens to prepare them for the sacrifices.

When the Day of Atonement came, thousands of us gathered to watch the High Priest begin the purification rite. The day was a rare one, with wisps of clouds in the sky and a dry, happy breeze. It seemed as if the LORD GOD prepared to welcome our return as HIS covenant people. We lined the cliffs above a rounded area where the stone was flat like a floor. Years before, the stone masons had carved severe columns into the cliffs, giving it the look of a rough temple, and they placed a great stone altar to one side. The tent makers among us had contrived a canvas HOLY OF HOLIES.

Slowly, the High Priest donned the plain white linens required by the LAW. The two goats were led to him, and by lot he determined the will of the LORD GOD, assigning one to HIM and the other to the demon Azazel. Then he tied a wooden tablet inscribed with *l'YHVH* to the head of the animal for the LORD GOD, and a wooden tablet inscribed with *la-azazel* to the head of the one for the demon.

In the days before, the High Priest selected an unmarried young man by lot to kill the bull. He was handsome and much like the bull in strength and vigor, which was also well-tended and magnificent. Its muscles shone in the sun through the black hide that was wrapped tightly upon him. Being used to handlers the bull was easily led onto the flatness of the stone where he stood at rest, snorting and clicking a hoof lazily against the rock.

The young man mounted the unsuspecting beast and with the quickness of a serpent pulled a long sword from his robes. Raising it with both hands above his head he pointed it directly down, and paused. The blade blazed in the sun and looked to be afire. The wind ceased and the clouds were motionless in the sky. We awaited in awe, our jaws agape and our blood stilled in our zeal for the sting of death.

He arched his body backward, bringing the sword even with the back of the bull, and lunging forward, drove it deeply between the shoulders. The surprised animal bellowed so loudly the rocks around us cracked as a great gasp escaped the people. The crazed beast began kicking up and down and threw the man into a wall where we heard his neck crack like the driest wood found in the desert. The bull kept roaring and thrashing about, spewing blood onto the men, women and children. A speechless chorus of desert souls, we watched as it staggered in drunken circles until it crashed upon the lifeless body of the young man, whose empty eyes were fixed upon the unseen. The High Priest, unmoved by the catastrophe, quickly walked over and slit the throat of the bull to let its thick black blood drain into a bronze bowl.

Leading the goat marked *l'YHVH*, the High Priest gravely walked to an area where the cliffs opened up into the desert and a low fire waited. The crowds watched as he took a stick with twined wools and a cup of water and placed them on the ground. Then he put the goat and an almond branch a few steps away. Two men bound the goat and slaughtered it, expertly slitting the throat and cutting its hind legs off, then flaying the hide and draining its blood into a second pan. After putting the hind legs in part of the hide and cutting the head off, the High Priest took the carcass and began cooking it over the fire. Using the rest of the hide, he wrapped it around the almond branch and then tied the front legs together with snares. In a moment of clumsiness he stumbled over the pan filled with the goat's blood, spilling some of it into the sand and onto his sandals. We looked on in amazement as he gathered up handfuls of the blood-clotted sand and dropped it into the pan.

"It is Adam!" croaked an old man.

The people began to murmur. "What strangeness is this?" they asked. "No good can come of this, a beardless man's death hangs upon the air," they said. "Yes, the angel of death has a thousand eyes, and blood has fallen upon the ground."

Servants appeared with bronze bowls filled with honey and oil bought from traders, and after digging a hole they poured the honey and oil in, along with a foreleg they hacked off from the goat. Then they placed the almond branch in the hole, hacked off the other foreleg, and also placed it in the hole.

The High Priest then led us back the temple area. Being a poor people we could manage nothing but a temple of heavy ivory canvas, and it was there that he took a panful of hot coals and two handfuls of aromatic incense and went inside the canvas curtain before the HOLY OF HOLIES. When we saw the smoke come from behind the curtain we knew that he had put the incense on the coals, and would go into the most holy room of the tent. Although we could not see him, we knew that he would sprinkle the grainy bull's blood on the East side of the cover, sprinkle it seven times on the front of the cover, and then do the same for the shrine. The priest came back outside and sprinkled blood on the horns of the stone altar, and sprinkled blood on the altar itself seven times. Then he took the blood of the goat and carefully repeated that which he did with the blood of the bull.

By now the sun was directly above us and the heat of the day was bearing down. Some of us lost interest in the slow, intricate movements of the High Priest, but we feared saying anything or even moving because this was the moment when our sins would be forgiven by the LORD GOD.

The High Priest then mixed the congealing blood of the bull and the goat in a third bowl and began the purification of the Tent of the Meeting. He made coarse smears on the curtain and then onto the four horns of a small incense altar, and sprinkled the remaining clumps of blood on the altar a final seven times.

And at last, it came time for evil to be expelled from our midst and sent to its owner. The High Priest walked slowly to the center of the stone circle. He was covered in blood and sand and dust, and the flecks of goat flesh hanging from his long beard gave him the look of a frenzied butcher.

The goat marked *la-azazel* was brought to him. He placed his stained hands upon it and began the confession. "I swear unto YOU, JEHOVAH, as YOUR covenant people, we have committed iniquities and wickedness, transgressed and sinned before YOU, YOUR people the House of Israel. I implore YOU, for the sake of JEHOVAH, forgive the sins that they have committed, transgressed, and sinned before YOU, YOUR people the House of Israel, for as it is written in the Torah of Moses YOUR servant:

> *For on this day shall atonement be made for you*
> *to cleanse you.*
> *You shall be clean before the LORD from all*
> *your sins.*

And the people standing nearest to the High Priest
and the goat, upon hearing the name of the LORD
GOD issuing from his mouth, fell to their knees, with
those behind them following in an outward ripple
of penitence saying, "Blessed be the name of HIS
kingdom's glory for ever and ever."

By now the goat was bucking and had to be
restrained by two men. The High Priest, whose hands
had seemed fused to the animal, pulled himself free
and fell away upon the stone. The beast was mad, its
eyes bulging and its mouth curled into a wild sneer
stretching the length of its snout back to its ears.
Its torso rigid, it went up and down on locked hind
and forelegs and started shaking its head to and fro,
splashing the foam from its mouth upon the shrieking
people who fell over one another as they tried to run
from the defilement.

After much begging and considerable bribing
we coaxed a wayfaring gentile into taking the crazed
animal into the desert to break its neck. Laughing, he
said, "Idiots! What are you so afraid of? I have never
seen such people act this way around a feebleminded
goat!" As soon as he took the tether the animal
became calm and acted just as a goat would. The
fool led it down the red desert road and out into the
wilderness while the High Priest said loudly, "Though
your sins be scarlet, they shall be as white as snow;

though they be red as crimson, they shall become like wool."

The High Priest then turned his attention to the remains of the bull and the other goat. The bull's carcass had begun to putrefy in the withering sun, and clouds of flies had gathered on the hide, in the nose and mouth, and in the wound. He slashed open its torso, and as he began scooping out handfuls of fat, the flies swarmed in a great black vortex above his head. "Beelzebub is among us!" hissed an elder. He did the same with the fat of the goat, and mixing the two together slathered them onto a charger on the altar. He set fire to the suet, and we all watched as the smoke made its way to heaven to refresh the LORD GOD.

We went to our dwellings, exhausted from the day's events. I fell into a deep sleep in my cave and did not awake until I felt my wife shaking me. "Listen," she hissed, "listen!" I heard the slow clattering of cloven hooves bouncing off the rock walls of the pass leading to the main part of our village. There was a loud bleating, deeply from the throat, that sounded like the cackling of a demon. As I looked out my door I saw my people holding their heads with their hands, their mouths open yet unable to scream as we looked at the goat *la-azazel* moving slowly through the town, pausing to look into each doorway.

I felt an abysmal fear grip the hearts of my people. The entire village was paralyzed. And then the endless screams began, swelling into a tumult of people barring their doors and windows shut. An old woman squatting in the middle of the passageway began a long, slow wail howling over and over, "We have been judged! We are cursed!" Another kept shouting, "We are as the uncircumcised!" A mob frenzied of men gathered, and dragged the High Priest from his home, threw ashes upon him, and beat him to death.

The wind began blowing from the east. It started as a low calmness, a barely perceptible yet vibrant silence, and it grew slowly in strength until it howled night and day and bore a scorching heat that burned the moisture out of the stones and the sand and flooded the streets with a river of dust. In the desiccation of our world the trees and plants withered into nothing and the animals began aborting, bawling as their jerking bodies threw huskish fetuses onto the desert floor where the roaring sand scoured the flesh from their pitiful carcasses, and the pitted bones were covered by the dunes that moved through like the waves of the sea.

Our women's breasts wasted and our children had no milk. The young wives were barren, and their husbands who lay atop them issued no seed, passing only clouded water. The deaths of young and old followed, and our days became endless lamentations for the dead and the living.

And into our community of despair returned the demons of old, demons we believed vanquished for all time when the LORD GOD made HIMSELF known to Moses by declaring, "I AM THAT I AM!"

"The Watchers are here!" we cried. "They have come again for our women! Our sacrifice to the brother of Semjaza has been rejected! Ours sins are upon us! What shall we do? What shall we do?" Fathers girdled their daughters for fear that the sons of the LORD GOD would return and mount them and reproduce the giants of old, and that a new time of sin and corruption would be unleashed upon the world.

An unkindness of ravens settled upon the village perched in dense black throngs about the cliffs and the doorways, their shit caked upon the doorways and passages, their throaty calls of alarm piercing the night, warning of the coming of evil, but in our blindness we did not listen. Then the vermin came; rats infested the streets and the storehouses, thousands upon thousands of tiny serpents scurried along the streets and in the shadows as if a single creature, yet scattering at the approach of a man and vanishing from sight even in the brightest of light. Our façade of fine columns and arches made by the hands of our noble craftsmen began to pit and crumble into dust as time withdrew from our midst.

Azazel's goat became our master, coming and going as he pleased, for we ran at his approach. He plundered homes, ate our food, and spread his filth and pollution among us. He molested our animals, mating with them at his will, and we waited in dread for the pregnant beasts to deliver their foul brood from the netherworld.

The old men gather in the meeting place and rail at one another, pulling on their beards like madmen as they speak the language of panic.

"I tell you, we should never have performed our own sacrifices. With our scriptures carried off into the wind like chaff we cannot tell precisely what the LAW requires. We have unleashed the fury of the LORD GOD!" shouted one.

"We have brought the wrath of the LORD GOD upon us by sacrificing to Azazel!" shouted another.

"Son of swine! It was no sacrifice to Azazel, the LORD GOD has rejected our confession," said a very old man whose beard nearly touched the ground.

Another old man bent over by the heaviness of his years says, "It is nothing we did. We witness the beginning of the WORLD TO COME."

In the silence of a pause I speak, "There must be an appeasement, and now we must appease the wrath of Azazael. We must make a new sacrifice." Everyone stops to listen.

"Can such a thing be done? Once his fury has been unleashed can it be appeased?" The old men argue back and forth about this.

"We must stop the power of Azazel, we must force it back below whence it came," bleated one of the men.

"But how do you force the wind down a hole?" asked another.

"Oh woe!"

"There must be blood," I say. "Pure blood."

"What we did, I will not tell you," Abba says; but he cannot resist himself so he tells the story.

"These dark things we do not know, so our most learned scholar must go down to the depths of the tunnels where we keep the remnants of our scrolls and after a while he emerges, his hair and beard splayed; 'ah,' he says, 'such secrets as I have found. Come close to me and I will tell you.'"

So the men with unmarried daughters draw lots and there is no surprise, the most beautiful is chosen and adorned with the best linens and perfumes we have, and two of the elders place their hands upon a ram and say, "Whosoever among the Watchers may become our ally this ram now stands ready, with its entrails, hearts, and limbs fattened and at the ready. From this time on, may the flesh of human beings be repugnant to Azazel and his demons, and to the

Watchers, and in the future may you be contented by this ram!"

The few hundreds of us that remain all bow behind the ram, and we then walk the ram and the woman, along with bread and wine, through the middle of the village to the edge of the desert. And then, in a low voice, an elder says, "Behold, the evil that was in this village for humans, and all other animals, what evil was here shall be taken out of our tribe by the ram and the woman. May whoever comes upon the ram and the woman take this evil upon itself!"

With the speed of a serpent two men stripped the woman of all her clothing. Shrieking, she tried to cover her nakedness but could not, and she was driven at sword point into the desert along with the ram and threatened unto death not to return.

In a few days fierce winds from the East began and brought a crushing storm; the rain came upon us like Nebuchadnezzar's armies, driving at us and throwing us about the streets. It was impossible to tell how long it lasted for the clouds blotted out the sun and the moon. The narrow passages of our village became swift rivers, and from the cliffs above we watched the heads of animals bobbing as they were swept out into the wilderness, taking the last of our hope with it.

"The LORD GOD promised that he would never again send a flood!" said the old men. "How do we deserve this misery?"

"It is not the LORD GOD who sends it," I said.

As the waters receded we found the scapegoat lying in the street, dead. The grizzled mat of its long hair was soaked, and blood oozed from its nose onto the worn rock of the road.

"It is dead, Azazel has died! Smell the smell; it is sickening! The demon has died, I tell you!" shouted one of the men.

"You are a thick-brained man, that is no demon. How can a demon die? That is the carcass of our sin, for evil has returned from its source and has lain its death down in a heap among us," said an elder.

The wailing began anew, "ahhhh, ahhhhh, ahhhhhh! Aieeee! We are a dead people! We are dead in the eyes of the LORD GOD!

An old man collapsed to the ground, tore at his robe, and began shaving his head. Muttering in gasps he said, "Shall evil befall a city and the LORD GOD not cause it? It is as the Prophets said, 'HE makes well-being and creates calamity.'"

Yowling in agreement, another old man shouted, "Is it not from the mouth of the MOST HIGH that good and bad come?"

The corpse of the goat remained in the street for no one dared touch it. As it rotted, its stench penetrated even the stone of the village. Maggots began crawling from its eyes, and nose, and anus, and flies began pouring from the holes they ate from inside the carcass.

We knew at last that the horn of salvation would not flourish, and that we were not among the sons of the House of David. Was any deliverance to be had? To whom could we appeal for some shred of comfort? We had observed the solemn rites as best we knew, but … this death that resides among us….

****

As the darkness of the morning surrendered to

81

the rising sun, the growing light revealed an obelisk at the edge of the village. The color of the deepest black of the night, we marveled at the perfection of its symmetry and how it stood at the height of two men. As word spread through the village, people began to gather and spoke in low, reverent murmurs. There was no script upon it, and its darkness glistened in the brilliant sunlight.

"It looks as if it has penetrated the face of the land," a boy said.

When the sun reached the highest part of the sky and cast no shadow, the obelisk moved. Startled, we jumped back and watched as its sides transformed into a dense wool that became a cape, and the pyramidion its hood. Some ran away, shouting, and as the hood slowly lifted we saw the deathly, pale face of a man. He had a very long chin and eyes the banded colors of onyx. Taking no notice of us he looked straight at the ground and slowly unfurled his arms until they were outstretched fully to either side, his hands opened and fingers separated. The cape drooped so low from his arms that they looked like wings.

Through black teeth he spoke, "People of Khorasaan, I have heard of your troubles and I have come to save you," he said. "I know of your misery, of how you, a blameless people, sent the goat into the wilderness as prescribed by the LAW, and have seen your faithfulness neglected by the LORD GOD."

He continued, "Your magic, for magic it is, does not have the power to save you and appease the wrath of the LORD GOD. I know the ways of time forgotten, of the ways of the days before men, of the secrets the LORD GOD has kept from HIS chosen people lest they become too powerful and as gods themselves."

This started murmuring in the crowd. "What is your name?" someone asked.

"My name is Assaph," he replied.

"A conjurer!" whispered an old man.

"I hear you, old man," said Assaph. "I am no conjurer. I am that I am!"

The crowd erupted. A man rent his gown, exposing his breast. "Blasphemer! Conjurer! Devil! Be done with us, and go back to the hole whence you came!" he screamed. The anger in the crowd increased, and some began to attack him. But his voice, not so much loud as clear and penetrating the very stones, overtook the noise of the people.

"Hear me people, the LORD GOD has turned HIS back to you; you are a doomed people. But there are ways, the ways of old, by which you may redeem yourselves and bring your souls back within HIS sight."

The protests continued but Assaph stood before us, unaffected. I moved closer to look at him and his head suddenly turned and he looked straight at me, and for a moment I saw in his eyes the depths of the welter and waste.

He said, "You, young man, you are a high and lofty thinker. Tell your people that they will greet destruction and death if they do not listen to me. You see that I speak truth."

I did not know what I saw. I was stunned that he had spoken to me, and I felt the wind of life escape my throat. I withdrew amid the noise, unnerved and confused.

Assaph remained at the edge of the village unmoved by the ferocious winds from the east, and

he eventually became as ordinary to us as the rock
and the sky and we paid him no heed. But day after
day he abided; silent, stolid, the center point of an
unseen vortex that swept up the world around us, for
as if the fate of our village were subject to his will evil
gathered itself together for a new attack upon us. The
earth shook terribly and the remnants of the facades
of Jerusalem fell to the ground as powder, exposing the
sheer rock faces and the black holes to our tunnels that
we scurried in and out of.

The wells ran dry and diseases attacked us; some
awoke to find themselves afflicted with leprosy, their
faces and hands swollen with weeping sores, and their
moans became the clamorous background of the daily
life of the village. Screaming, the children bolted from
the shuffling monsters, and the stench of their rotting
flesh and their pollution demanded that we drive them
away and into the desert. And still others developed
the scales of serpents, and they too we drove into
the desert for fear that the adversary possessed their
bodies and their souls. Entire families were struck blind
and staggered in unison with the diseased, howling
at their misfortune and groping among the stones at
noonday, and believing that the demon of blindness
had come upon us we covered what little open water
we had so he could not rest upon it at night. Women
in childbirth were attacked by other women, and men
and women were overcome with desire such that they
panted openly in their copulation. The blood of the
unclean women that had the blackness of the abyss
smelled horribly as it trickled into the streets.

In this hollow place we became a people of dust.
We were near absolute death. I do not know how
or why but I was one of the few passed over by the

demons that had invaded us. I knew not what else to do, and so I gathered my strength, overcame my fear, and ventured out to meet Assaph.

"I knew you would return," he said. "I told you to tell your people that they would meet their end if they did not heed my words. Are they now ready to listen?"

My mouth tasted of ashes, my organs had shriveled from the lack of food and water; I barely had the strength to speak. "Yes," I stuttered, "I will speak with them. But I must know, do you mean to harm us? Can you save us?"

"How can I harm you? Do you not already dwell in the dust? Tell your people I shall save them."

Many of the elders had either died or were half-mad from disease and the lack of food and water. "What choice have we?" the few sane ones said. "The LORD GOD has forgotten us, HE has broken faith with us. Perhaps if we can survive a while longer we may find a way to appease HIM. Tell Assaph we will follow."

I returned to Assaph and, with the fatigue of the forgotten man, listened to his instructions. "You must cleanse the land of its sins. You are now the High Father. Obey me and death will pass by you and all," he said.

In my mindlessness I began to gather the materials for a sacrifice. Wood was scarce and I trekked through the desert for days, carrying back bits of sticks and dried brush. I secretly began building an altar on a sand hill, and after finding the necessary firestone and cleaver I seized a young boy from his feeble parents. He had curly brown hair that fell to his shoulders, and his bones were fleshed from the food his parents had denied themselves for his sake. I bound his arms behind him at the wrists and again tightly at his upper arms so his bare chest was taut. After stuffing filthy rags into his mouth I then bound his legs, and carrying him over my shoulder to the altar threw him upon it. By now his eyes were bulging as he tried to scream through the rags stuffed in his mouth, and as he strained to free himself, I began the prayer given to me by Assaph.

"LORD GOD of the storm, you who ride upon the clouds and bring thunder and lightning, prince lord of the earth, prince of glory and the kingdom, son of man to whom dominion is given, that all peoples, nations, and languages should serve you, your kingdom shall not pass away and shall not be destroyed," I stammered.

We began limping around the altar in a broken dance of fatigue calling out, "LORD GOD of the storm, hear us, answer us. We are a dead people, it is you who must deliver us from this evil," and while chanting this over and over we began slashing ourselves on the insides of our arms at the moment prescribed by Assaph, slinging our blood across the altar and the boy, who was by now screaming mightily and thrashing against the bindings.

I raised the cleaver above my head with both arms fully extended and waited, hoping for a voice to call from above, listening for a laugh from the LORD GOD above calling a stop to this madness, awakening us all from this barren dream we were living, restoring us to our place among the chosen. But nothing came, and I felt my very own breath of life escape from me.

I drove the cleaver into his breastbone and it burst open like ripened fruit in a summer basket, and there before my eyes was his heart pounding in the frenzy of the moment. His neck was swollen with screaming and terror, and becoming rigid and unable to control himself his seed ejaculated upon the dirty linens that covered his body.

Heeding Assaph's instructions I took the cleaver and carefully slit the beating heart down its length. The blood began pumping into the cavity around his heart, filling it slowly and then running over his sides on to the sticks and brush of the altar. By then the boy had ceased his struggles and lay still, so I dipped my hands in his blood and smeared it across my face and arms, and did so for anyone who would step forward so that we stood as an inhuman, blooded tribe whose stark white eyes burned with the knowledge of good and evil. Striking the firestone made the wood come alive, and I watched as the smoke of burning flesh and blood and bits of ash made its way to the heavens where I hoped the fragrance would please the God who received it.

The entire village fell into the death of sleep. I do not know how many days it was before we awoke, but when I returned to the altar nothing remained. Everything had turned to ash and blown away into the wilderness.

I seek out Assaph, who remains at his corner. "You have done well," he says. "And now, it is time to prepare for the next sacrifice."

I am stunned. "You said nothing about more than one sacrifice," I manage to say. "You told me that we should follow your direction and sacrifice a male child. More than this we cannot do."

"Your head is nothing but an empty chest of boards," he retorts. "I never told you that one sacrifice would be sufficient. Die if you will, it is nothing to me.

Follow me, and you will be redeemed."

What choice have we? To whom should we sacrifice? Our memory as a people has left us; we do not know who we are. Somewhere in the time before history we were among the chosen. Are we now the children of Esau whom the LORD GOD rejected in HIS secret counsel? Are we now among the cursed?

And so begins the ritual extermination of my people. What little restraint we possess blows away into the desert with the ashes of the boy's sacrifice. An elder takes his first son for a burnt offering on the wall; still others take their sons and set fire to them in the valley. We sacrifice our sons and daughters to the demons and pour out their innocent blood upon the powder of the earth where it becomes wet, polluted clay so at night we hear the cries of our children cursing us from the ground.

When the heat of our fever burns itself out we stop, realizing in the remnants of our destruction the abomination we have become. Enraged, we make our way to Assaph to destroy him, and as we gather around him to kill him he halts us with a word.

"*YHVH*," he says quietly, and simply, and perfectly.

The speaking of the nameless name arrests us; it is a word we know but have never heard, and in that moment the dread of THE MOST HIGH GOD passes into us and takes its place in our hearts. We cannot move and there is no air or light or smell; there is naught but Assaph and those who stand near him in the stillness.

Assaph speaks. "Why do you wish to harm me? I have caused no troubles. Do you not know who you are? Look, where is your shadow? You have no shadow, it is you who are a shadow, a shadow of dust.

That box of bones Abba's Abba resides in? It is filled with dust. The breath you draw is as empty as the breath of the beasts."

"But we are the chosen of the LORD GOD," I say.

"Indeed you are HIS chosen; chosen for death. You are nothing but food for the LORD GOD'S worms. Your bones will be a feast for maggots and come the day of wrath, you will be as nothing; the wind will whistle through the holes left in your bones and your joints will clatter with corruption. The dead know nothing. You know nothing."

"This I do not believe, for the LORD GOD is good."

"Good? Oh yes, HE is good. But evil? Can the LORD GOD make good and not make evil? Who is this god that creates both? Has not the LORD GOD sent you, a blameless people, to die in this wasted place?"

"That cannot be," and I whisper, "Jehovah-Jireh."

"There is no deliverance here, and you do not answer me," Assaph says. "Whence comes this evil of sin and guilt? What do your scriptures say about such?"

"They say nothing."

"Yes, the words of the LORD GOD are silent."

And quietly I say, "There is only one GOD."

"In this you are right, but you have no answers to my questions and there are still more to be asked. Can it be that there is a chosen people, yet also those who are passed by? Have you not been passed by?"

To these things I had no answers. All I could do was ask the question, "Who are you?"

"I am HIS brother the twin," Assaph answered.

"What?"

89

"Do you not know who I am? Did you not send the goat into the desert to summon me? I came from Hermon to see who asked for me and what do I find? This forsaken tribe of broken Jews who butcher the Torah and spill worthless blood upon the land. How pitiful you are. You send the goat into the desert but do not know your own magic."

There is an absolute silence upon my people, for the dread of THE LORD GOD has passed from our hearts into our livers and our kidneys and we know that judgment stands before us. Assaph changes himself in an instant, revealing himself as the demon we now know him to be, and how can I describe this beast? He is hideous, and his living flesh seems to decay before us and fall to the ground in scraps. His skin is blackness itself, and he has great claws made for digging through the earth. His mouth is a gaping maw that shows the fangs of a serpent and his stench fills the air and chokes us. But his eyes, the eyes of the very abyss itself are unchanged.

He cries out, his great chest heaving, "Do you now know me? Do you not see he to whom you sacrificed the goat? Behold! Azazel stands before you!"

We throw ourselves to the ground and await death from the crushing grip of his great claws as he stamps around above us, and as we begin our descent into dust I whisper to my people the words from the prophet:

"The end has come upon my people Israel; I will never again pass by them.

The songs of the temple shall become wailings in that day, declares the LORD GOD.

So many dead bodies!

They are thrown everywhere!

Silence!"

The Last Anchorite

Truly, I say to you, all sins will be forgiven the children of man, and whatever blasphemies they utter, but whoever blasphemes against the Holy Spirit never has forgiveness, but is guilty of an eternal sin.

MARK 3:28-9 (ESV)

With gratitude to Colmán Ó Clabaigh OSB.

Rhythmically, she stamps her bare feet into the freezing mud as she huffs frail ghosts of breath into the dank night air. The demons howl as they ride down upon the winds of the North, hurtling themselves endlessly against her stone cell as she lifts her knees to her chest over and again, forcing her legs down in a stationary march.

— I am so cold. That bitch of a peasant girl has left me for dead. Foul wench! A curse upon her! I have no fire, I have no food or water. I have nothing but my Lord and Saviour. Oh Lord! Do not strike me in your anger, or punish me in your wrath. Be gracious to me, for I am weak....

— Prayer and penance, prayer and penance, prayer and penance....

Her knees rising to her chest, her footprints grow deeper as she tramps; the January muck rises stiffly between her splayed toes and the earth reverberates beneath her steps such that the columns of rock in the world below shake and pieces of stone loosen and clatter down into the endless hollows. The spirits perched on the ledges listen, their heads cocked to the side.

— Her death march, one remarks.

— Tell the adversary, says another.

— Depart from me! You workers of evil! shrieks the anchorite. The Lord hears my weeping!

She has forgotten her name. Her purple velvet robe is rotted into a ragged lace, and it whirls about

her like a tattered wraith as the North wind swirls
inside her cell. She is accustomed to her stench and
her hair, gray-black and straggled, reaches almost
to her knees. Her skin is weather-beaten into deep
wrinkles and folds, and her nails are broken and dirty
from scraping out her grave with her hands.

Her tongue licks at her cracked lips as she prays
between huffs.

— Jesus, my light.
— Jesus, my joy.
— Jesus, my peace.
— Have mercy on me.

She stops, her robe comes to rest, and she wheezes
her words.

— Today is Wednesday … I believe …. grief dims
my eyes.

— But you, O Lord, how long? Set my soul free.

A clacking of stones being stacked sounds in her
mind: the village workers are chiseling away the cobble
that covers the door of the cell where the eremite
before her had died: the body had fallen into the
grave she dug for herself and the commoners were
filling it with the earth, the body a palimpsest upon the
soulless husks of those who had lived and died in the
cell before her.

Then a child-novice at the convent, she watched
as the Bishop, crowded in the cell with his servants,
performed the Mass of the Dead.

— *Memento etiam Domine et eorum Maria qui nos
processerunt,* the Bishop intoned.

The blue smoke of the incense exhaled from the
solitary window, lingered, and rose into the sky. The
group of novices lowered their heads and prayed:

— O Lord. Deliver her life….

— Save me for the sake of your faithful love, the anchorite murmurs in her cell.

The cell stood empty for years, a landmark for the novices and the nuns, and its single eye always stared at the anchorite as she walked to her labors in the fields while the nuns and novices chanted,

— Joy comes in the morning…. You have turned my laments into dancing.

— Blessed is the one whose disobedience is forgiven, whose sin is covered, the anchorite whispers.

— Prayer and penance, prayer and penance, prayer and penance… happy is a man when the Lord lays no guilt to his account….

— Then I declared my sin, my guilt I did not conceal… I will confess my disobedience to the Lord…. she wheezes.

She met the young man while working in the fields. Her novice's habit was no hindrance to him, and he came around when she was alone and in prayer.

— Let me show you love, he said.

— I have the love of Christ, she said.

— But Christ cannot love you as I can, let me show you love.

— But the Holy Ghost watches us, she said.

— To Hell with the Holy Ghost, he whispered.

— To Hell with the Holy Ghost, she repeated as she succumbed and made the words of evil sound, and went to lay with him.

The man disgusted her, but she thought little of it until Sunday Mass when the priest gave the homily.

— There is but one sin that Christ in His infinite love cannot pardon, and that is the sin of the blasphemy of the Holy Ghost. Those who blaspheme the Holy Ghost have no hope, and Hell awaits them when they leave this world.

She was stricken there in the church; her sisters gathered about her as a flittering blue and white covey, certain that Satan had assaulted their most pious and beloved as a show of his power and wickedness. When she awoke the prioress stood over her.

— Child, are you well?

Supine, she was motionless.

— Child? Can you not speak?

She lay there, paralytic, for weeks in the stone light of the convent unable to speak, and the blue pall of terror was about her.

— I am going to Hell, she thought.

— For eternity.

— There is no hope.

She eventually asked for the Bishop, who sent an assistant to inquire about the matter.

— Holiness, the novice wishes to go into the cell at the Church of the Blessed Virgin.

The Bishop paused over his plate of sausages and cheeses.

— Whatever for? he asked.

— She will not say other than she desires the life of prayer and penance.

— Hmmm. You know the last one in there, I forget her name, went completely insane and I won't have that again. She shrieked and howled and clawed at the walls for weeks and the poor priest couldn't hear himself say Mass. And I can't have someone who is a drain on our resources. There simply isn't enough to spare for someone shut up in a cell who can't go out into the fields. Still, the right person could be an inspiration to the commoners, to show them what real obedience and piety looks like. Has anyone else

95

expressed any interest?

— No, holiness.

— Well then, let us speak with her and we shall see if she is suitable.

When the novice entered the room the Bishop thought,

— The woman has the look of death about her.

— My daughter tell me, why do you wish to become an anchorite?

—Holiness, my life of sin calls me to deep penance and prayer for all of my days.

— Is there something you wish to confess?

— No, holiness, my sin is the sin of my being.

— Sin crouches at our door, the Bishop cautioned.

— I must rule over it, my salvation is at stake, she replied.

— Have you a patron?

— Yes, holiness, Thomas Fitzgerald has agreed to sponsor me.

The Bishop's eyes glimmered.

— The Earl of Desmond? How did you acquire such a noble and learned patron?

— He is a cousin, holiness. He has fixed a corrody for me.

— Then I must personally thank him for his graciousness. I will write to him directly, and of course my child, we gladly accede to your profession and shall have you installed as soon as you have the funds for the work necessary to prepare the cell. And a tithe to the diocese would be most welcome, too.

— Thank you, holiness.

As the preparations with the cell went, so it went with the novice. While the nuns and novices walked to the fields amid the clang of the hammers and chisels, the jangle of the church bells, and the crashing of the blacksmith's hammer on the anvil they chanted,

— The Lord is a lover of justice and will not forsake his loyal servants. I will praise thee again and yet again…because you have redeemed me. All day long my tongue shall tell of your righteousness.

Walking with them, her scythe over her head, the novice prayed to herself, softly,

— There is no health in me because of my sin, my iniquities are a load heavier than I can bear, my wounds fester and stink because of my folly.

The Bishop's clever masons rebuilt the cell to ten feet long, ten feet wide, and ten feet high, laid a slab of stone for her bed, and placed a piss-pot in the corner. They set the mortar between the stones, placed new iron bars in the window upon the world, and hid crucifixes in the walls to form an unseen chain of crosses to repel the demonic assault that was surely to come. And, should she go mad and require that the cell be breached, shackles were fixed to the walls. A long, cold slit she could but put her fingers through was her squint to see into the church.

As the day of her enclosure approached, she fasted and prayed, and kept a vigil in her room at the convent the night before while the taper burned quietly in the church. The next morning the Bishop, stiff with the dignity of his office, led a procession of priests, vicars, and oblates, followed by a stream of nuns, their sunlit coifs aflutter in the light breeze. In their midst the novice stepped slowly, dressed in a purple velvet cape over a plain cloth dress, a rope tied around her neck and her wrists bound. Her shaven head was dull in the sunlight.

The nuns sang,

— The Lord has been my strong tower, and my rock of refuge. Let us raise a joyful song to Him, and shout the triumph of our salvation.

The novice whispered,

— Wash away my guilt and cleanse me of my sin.

The Bishop raced through the Mass, laid the Eucharist upon her tongue, and then bade her to prostrate herself upon the floor of the Church as he began,

— *Veni, Creator Spiritus,* take your servant Ana, keep her holy and free of sin, may she keep a tidy cell and not grumble about her food and drink, keep her chaste and make her days full with prayer and penance.

The aspergillum spattered the holy water across her clothing in dark blotches and she felt a little upon her face, which chilled her. Then she said,

— I, sister Ana, give myself to the mercy of God as an ancresse in His service and shall live by the rule of an ancresse and here in the presence of your Holiness Father Bishop, I commit my body and being to the Father.

The church roll was brought to her, and pricking her finger with a pin she made a cross upon the page with her blood and recited the words the Bishop had given her,

— My law is the law that regulates my heart, my law is love.

The Bishop led the procession from the church and she stepped upon the earthen floor of the cell while everyone gathered at the entrance, and the Bishop prayed,

— Bless O Lord this bridal chamber and this your servant Ana living in it, and may she remain in

your love with fasting, prayers and vigils and may she
day by day build up the clergy and people of God by
leading a pure and religious life until the end of her
life. Amen.

He slammed the door shut, threw the bolt, and
placed a lock upon the latch. The masons quickly
placed the stones over the door, and the Bishop
charged a constable to remain there until the mortar
had set fast.

So began the days of her life in her cell. Cut
cruelly low, the knee-high squint forced her onto all
fours in the chill of the morning so she could see the
pale, perfectly round Eucharist held aloft by the priest
during Mass in the dim morning light.

— *Accépit panem in sanctas ac venerábiles manus suas...*
the priest said, and bowed slightly.

— *Accipíte et manducáte ex hoc omnes hoc est enim corpus
meum....*

The priest thrust communion at her through the
squint saying,

— *Corpus Christi.*

— Amen.

She sat on her stone bed and let the host linger
on her tongue where it tingled as it dissolved, and
returned to the squint and moved her head back and
forth across the narrow cut, straining to see a fragment
of a beatific face in the rose window or a portion of a
hand in repose among the polished folds of a marble
robe, and there she remained until the last candles
were extinguished and she looked into the void.

She gazed with intimacy at each stone in the cell:
she loved their cut edges and dense crystalline faces;
she knew them all and fancied giving them names but
did not lest she be thought mad; still, every stone spoke

to her and at times they sang to her in a chorus of granite voices,

— Prayer and penance, prayer and penance, prayer and penance....

Then she paced round and round in her cell making a shallow, lemniscate path in the earthen floor while saying,

— Prayer and penance, prayer and penance, prayer and penance, and moving betwixt and between the squint and its slitted view of the church and her window upon the world, grasping the bars high on the window and pulling herself to the tips of her toes, pressing her round face to the cold iron and looking at the world and the moon and the stars, and watching the cycles of the seasons swirl by. The low, maddening Fall sun set the cell ablaze and seemed to hasten too slowly to its setting so that she longed for the night, and then in the depths of the darkness prayed for the sun to again rise. The biting cold of Winter and swelter of Summer made the marrow in her bones ache and boil so that the new breath of Spring or the coolness of the Fall evenings gave her comfort for a while until the Winter and the Summer again made themselves known.

In the cold of the night she stood with her feet in a bucket of water, fasted for days to know the pain of the flesh, or lay on her bed supine and without movement to mimic the body in death. Her rosary became her scourge, and she flogged her shins and ankles into a chaotic latticework of welts and rosy, weeping flesh, and let the flies and bugs crawl upon her wounds for nourishment and lay their eggs that became wriggling larva that fell to the ground and transformed into a cloud that slowly whirled above her.

And every day, her death always before her eyes, she scraped a little at her tomb she set below the squint so that in time she knelt lower and lower in her grave as she gazed upon the Eucharist, not knowing that the anchorites before her had all made their graves in the same place.

Her holiness became famous, and it was said that Mary herself came and visited the Anchorite and that the prayers of the recluse were heard by Christ, who often cured those souls for whom she sought His grace. But the days were also for talk and rumors. The village women came to the window and spoke in whispers, asking for prayers or advice, or telling the Anchorite the news of the Parish and the illicit loves and conflicts and despair of its people. At nights rough men came who stared through the window or clawed at the stones trying to find a way in, and muttered curses at their failures.

This holiness drew many visitors from afar, and those who would seek favor or gossip and make their offerings alarmed the Bishop, who was at once torn and relieved by the seeming prosperity of the Anchorite. He had taken great care to assure that the Anchorite was fully supported so she would not be a burden upon the diocese but now he heard of geese, chickens, and baskets of bread and vegetables and cheeses that she bartered, and there were rumors that the people gave her gold and silver and jewels for safekeeping so that the man was tinged by jealousy that her fortunes seemed to exceed his own, and he imposed a strict rule that she was to possess nothing, and that her sustenance was limited to a single visit a week from her patron or his agent, who was allowed to bring her enough to sustain her, and nothing else.

— Remember your vows, the Bishop's fat, boyish vicar told her, and the Bishop says do not tarry at the window or you will become distracted.

The floor of her cell became a desert for single combat with her adversary. She had been warned about his deceits.

— He will come to you in many guises, said a priest.

— Guard your heart and body, said another.

— Child, the Prioress said, the first years are an easy burden, it is when you have been there for ten or fifteen or twenty years or more that the true battles begin…. You will think Jesus has forgotten you, but He has not. He tests you for your own good. All the ends of the earth have seen the victory of our God.

In the sixth hour of the day the demons began to appear, at first one or two, then flocks: small, hideous demons that roosted on the stones in the cell, chattering, flinging insults and their shit at her and each other, and flitting from stone to stone with ease.

— *Verbum caro factum est!* she cried to expel them, but they jeered.

— Stupid bitch! they howled. No one listens to you.

— Is all of you shriveled like your skin?

— We know this one's sins, don't we? We'll be around to collect her soul when her time comes, said another.

— Soon the maw of her grave will devour her and she will live in the blackness.

When the demons finally left she lay upon her bed, and a torpor came over her so that she cared nothing for herself or her prayer and penance.

— My days vanish like smoke and my body is

burnt; I am wracked.... The choking sulphur, I won't
be able to breathe, the darkest dread in my bones and
muscles, or endless screams and clamor so I shout until
I cannot shout anymore—how long does that last?
Forever? What is forever? Hopeless, I have no hope—I
have tears but no hope, and it is me—I did this; I killed
myself with my flesh and my mouth, my flesh and my
mouth are my enemies and I am death.

— And what of my life? If I had married or felt
a child move in my womb? Pushed my hands into the
earth or breathed the scents of the flowers and herbs,
how I loved those smells, or looked upon the whole
sky and felt the rain upon my face or the sun upon my
skin, or planted the fields under a full moon or swam
in a river? Heard the laughter of my children and held
them, felt their hearts beating and heard the sound of
their breathing? How might that have been? To have
had even a single child for my immortality? Out of the
depths I cry to you, O Lord! O Lord, hear my voice.
Every morning I flood my grave with tears.

She brushed a dry tear from her eye with the back
of her hand and opened her rheumy eyes to see a tiny
demon in her face.

— Cunt! Your cunt is shriveled! No babies for
you!

She swatted, but it was too quick.

— Ha! Bitch! You'll have to do better than that!

— *Verbum caro factum est*, she whispered.

She would look at her Bible with no profit or
scrape a little at her grave, or try and mend her
clothes, but always, always, from deep inside her
the wailing began, the long, low, vibrant silence of
a wailing that lasted for days and quietly shook the
ground in her cell in a way that she alone felt.

In the night a stone loosed from the parapet of
the church and smashed onto the roof of her cell,
shattering the fever of her dreams. It happened again
the next night, and a few weeks later the fat vicar
returned to the cell and announced,

— The Bishop has died. So has the Earl of
Desmond.

— I thank the Lord for the goodness of the Earl
of Desmond and weep for the death of his Holiness. I
give thanks the Earl of Desmond has provided for me
in his estate.

— Do not be so certain, I am told that the Earl
of Desmond died penniless from his dissolute life.
The Bishop made no provision for you either, so you
had best see to other arrangements because there is
nothing to spare for you. And there is other news, the
great Julian of Norwich has died and a new manner of
thought makes its way across the land. Man, not God
is the center of thought. You are the last of your kind,
you who imprison yourselves for the sake of God.

— I am a prisoner of myself, she thought. Enter
not into judgment with your servant, O Lord, for no
one living is righteous before you.

The life of the place was let out of it. The bustle of
the commoners disappeared and the seasons of the year
no longer moved with any sense of order, for it seemed
as though God had shaken time and loosed the world
from its axis. She hardly noticed the permanent eclipse
of the sun: the black moon had stopped upon it and the
strangled ghost of the sun's corona cast her cell in a deep,
relentless gray. The new bishop ordered the cathedral
closed so the priest said goodbye and God Bless, and
without ceremony locked the doors. The squint looked
into nothing but a dank stone void.

The peasant girl had quit coming, her food and water dwindled, and the winds from the North were gathered into a deep roar that blasted her cell. Her knees were knotted with pain and she could not stamp for warmth anymore, so she sat upon her bed and listened. The demons, riding upon the winds, were yowling and screaming, crying out for her soul as they slammed onto the cell, trying to smash their way in.

— Who are you, you children of men and angels? Your faces are delusions and your horns are illusions; you are darkness. You are not light. Get behind me....

Smelling death, a few ravens landed close by on a withered tree and began watching.

— We will wrestle with the angels for that soul, one of them says.

There was nothing for her to do but wait, so she spent her days upon her bed, a recumbent effigy in the gray light. The chill air saturated her bones and her robe was a careless shroud of corrupt velvet.

— O Lord, heal me, for my bones are in agony. Prayer and penance ... prayer ... and ... penance, here it is, death comes, and the cold, it is so cold, I have counted for nothing, so this is how it is when death comes, alone, cold, hungry, and salvation ... where is it? Where is my salvation? Where is....

She heard a rustle outside the window and pulled herself up to see a small village boy kicking at the dirt and stones and dead leaves.

— Boy! Boy! she said.

— Boy! Come here!

Frightened by the apparition the boy set to bolt away.

— Come here boy, I won't harm you.

— Are you a witch? he asked.

105

— I am no witch, I am a woman who is dying. Summon the priest. I tell you, summon the priest!

She returned to her bed and waited, and more ravens gathered on the leafless trees and the low, croaking *prruk prruk* of the conspiracy swelled into a clattering chorus that sounded distant and hollow in the winter day. The elder among them took an accounting of their actions, to which one of them spoke up.

— Soon I will bring you the soul of the one in the hermit's cell.

— Oh?

— Yes, she dies, and she has a sin which she has not confessed, and she will take that sin to her grave. Then I shall have her soul.

Eventually, the priest came with the key to the lock and waited impatiently while the masons chiseled at the stone, but they had done their work too well because the wall would not give and the blows bounced off, and but for the presence of the holy man they would have taken to swearing and drinking. But the priest soon fell asleep, so the masons sent for sledges and whiskey and food, for they believed they might have to camp for the night. In their eagerness to get into the cell they set up a two-man team to work the sledges with alternating strokes while a third held a large chisel. But they drank too much whiskey and a man swinging a sledge missed and struck the man holding the chisel in the head, nearly killing him. The uproar awakened the priest, who when upset was himself given to strong language and making oaths, and he swore terribly at the drunken masons.

Impatient with their foolishness, the priest picked up a sledge and chisel and found a place he thought closest to the top of the door to the cell and started at the wall. At the first blow the hammer pinged loudly and popped back off the head of the chisel and nearly struck him in the face; undeterred, he struck again and again at the exact same point until he felt the mortar crack in the slightest way, and this encouraged him on until bits started flying.

He reached a place where he could see a small hollow behind the stones, so he determined to open the area up and after a few more blows a small, blackened crucifix popped out, followed by another and another, and rather than let them fall to the ground he caught them and placed them inside his cassock. The wall then seemed to start to dissolve, and he easily knocked away the rest of the stones until the door lay exposed in full before him. Its timbers had become dark and the massive iron hinges were so black that the priest could hardly see them. He produced the key from among the folds of his cassock and placing it in the lock, prepared to turn it with all his strength, but the key moved smoothly and the lock opened with a simple click.

The masons crowded around the door and the priest commanded them to stand back, and as he opened the door his knees buckled from the stench of the filth inside.

— Dear God, he thought, this reeks of corruption.

He made the sign of the cross in the air with his open right hand as he entered, and covered his mouth and nose with a scented cloth held by the other. But he had to push himself into the stillness; a soft, uterine resistance surprised him, so he used his right hand to rupture its membrane and wade inside.

107

— I cannot see a thing, he thought.

He allowed himself a moment to become accustomed to the cell, and his eyes came into focus and he breathed the stench deeply, first through his mouth to avoid choking and then deeply through his nose until his lungs were filled with the smells of earth and urine and shit and death.

It was then that he saw the Anchorite. He made out her dim, supine form atop her stone bed and he could hear a soft wheezing.

— Who … who is it? she asked. Elisha? Is that you? Prayer and penance, prayer and penance, prayer and penance....

— She's delirious, the priest thought.

— I am the priest, you sent for me because you are dying. I am here to prepare you for death.

The half-sober masons, alarmed by the smell and the gloom inside the cell, packed up their tools and fled. The ravens began to alight quietly on the cell and listen.

The priest heard naught but her soft wheezing, and stepping closer he saw her shabbiness and the crags of her face and her unblinking eyes looking directly into his. Looking away he said,

— Woman, I haven't all day. It is time for me to hear your last confession and administer the rites. Have you confessed all of your sins? Be careful that you do, for your time here is at an end and a merciless judgment awaits you.

She started heaving, and between sobs managed to say,

— I have but one unconfessed sin Father; in my youth I cursed the Holy Spirit. I have spent a life in repentance. I was a young girl, I know that the Lord is

108

God, he is good and his love endures forever.

— Father … I ask you … am I saved?"

The priest said nothing: his face was as silent as the stones of the cell. He put the oil he brought with him back in its pouch.

— I'll not waste the final rites and holy chrism on her, he thought. She's done. She's a fraud. All these years her life was a lie. A curse upon her, letting people think she's a holy person. Her soul was stained black with sin for all time. She knew it.

— Let everything that has breath praise the Lord, she said in the chill of the cell. The Anchorite exhaled her soul, and with the last pulse of her heart her body relaxed. The priest paused for a moment, and did not close her pale, perfectly round eyes.

— There it is, he thought.

The ravens, by now crowded around the window, tensed and burst in all directions.

The Lake of
Fire Church

AHAB SON OF OMRI became king of Israel in
the thirty-eighth year of Asa king of Judah, and he
reigned over Israel in Samaria for twenty-two years.
He did more that was wrong in the eyes of the LORD
than all his predecessors. As if it were not enough
for him to follow the sinful ways of Jeroboam son of
Nebat, he contracted a marriage with Jezebel daughter
of Ethbaal king of Sidon, and went and worshipped
Baal....

1 Kings 16:29-31 (NEB)

Things were heating up at the Lake of Fire Church. Ahab Bale prepared for the sermon of sermons, the achievement that would crown his years in service of the Word. The world desperately needed him: the prophecies were being fulfilled. Britain had broken away from Europe, Russia and China were secretly joining forces to make a 200-million-man army, Iran was set to dominate the Middle East, and the President had designated Jerusalem as the capital of Israel. It had all been foretold, it was all there in the Bible, the strongmen in Russia and China, the butcher Duterte in the Philippines, all men of lawlessness, all men the Bible predicted … if you possessed the knowledge, the key to understanding its secrets.

And America. The country had disassembled into a frightening vortex of sin. The violence, the drugs, the coming economic collapse, the corruption of government. The faggots had begun their subversion of American society in earnest. They saw themselves as the knowing arbiters of culture and taste: heterosexuals were clumsy, stupid, and uninformed. Divorce and abortion were rampant. Soulless clones threatened to stampede the horizon. The myth of economic happiness had become the new idolatry. Moral lawlessness was the order of the day; collapse was inevitable. Every clamoring constituency demanded rights; no one wanted responsibility for anything. People felt marginalized. People were scared. People craved leadership, a voice, a light … the plain truth. But few people clearly saw the truth, and the truth was that his church was under attack.

Bale knew the truth, the God-given truth. He would give it to them. In three days he would mount the new pulpit cast into a bronze chariot, don his brass armor and helmet, hold his shining sword on high, and preach to his followers that the grand and final catastrophe was near, that good was losing the war with evil, and that something must be done before an angry God revealed himself in his terrible wrath and destroyed everything. This was a war, a holy war, and only Bale could command the morality that would stay God's vengeance. They would follow Bale as he rode his blazing chariot across the heavens.

The heat of the summer night burned at the ministry building. Looking through the wrought iron work on the windows, Bale saw the grain fields in the distance and the nearby vineyard. The broken silhouettes of the corn stalks were lit by spurts of lightning in the dry solstice sky; the blackened grapevines were contorted on the trellises and the bunches of withered grapes looked like gnarled fists. There was a time when the sight would have unnerved him, but no more. He saw it for what it was, yet another sign of the end of days. Still....

He pulled the note from his drawer and looked at the penciled scrawl: "Except by my command, there shall be no dew or rain or water. The sky is locked." He clenched his jaw and thought about the months of drought, the desiccated fields, and the deep fissures in the earth where the lake had once been. The entire ministry and staff watched as the last of the fish flopped in the mud, gulping the sludge and pushing it through their gills as they choked and became still.

The stench of rotted fish lingered for weeks.

Bale's staff found the note tacked to the front door of the church three years before and he kept it as a curiosity and an amusement, the work of an obvious madman, but then he did not throw it away because the derelict began to appear on the security cameras, staring directly into them, motionless, his deep eyes unblinking. In one photo he squatted and pointed to the words he had made by pressing small stones into the earth, "My God is Jehovah." Here and there the security patrols found small altars where a rabbit or a dove had been sacrificed; the small, unburnt parts of the animals were lying in the ashes, matted with blood and mud, and they found a jar of meal and a jug of oil for making bread. Once, the crazed man ran boldly in the front of Bale's motorcade as it returned from a trip. "Run him down," Bale said, but as soon as the driver stamped the accelerator the man darted away into the woods.

And the wolves. There had been no wolves in the area for over a century, and the farmhands began to find the carcasses of cattle and sheep torn to pieces, their bones crushed by powerful jaws and their guts scattered across the ground. Even now he could see the pack of black animals in the fractured light, their red eyes glowing and focused upon him. There was no telling how much money he had spent trying to kill them. Traps, hunters, poison, nothing worked. They seemed to defy death, and the photos from the game cameras always showed the alpha male looking directly into the camera at Bale, at least until the wolves ripped the cameras from the trees and shredded them. "Satan and his minions," he thought.

Drumming his tumid fingers on the glossy

rosewood desk, he stared at the concentric circles radiating from an ocular knot in the grain. The desk was a prize, milled from a single unblemished tree said to have been the finest in all of Madagascar and felled by the hands of the faithful. He knew that the tree had grown for him and only him, a seed deliberately fallen upon the jungle floor years before his birth, a seedling fighting its way through the darkness of the canopy into the light, and now a mature and perfect tree whose stillness formed an altar for the Important Work ordained for his ministry. When he looked at the knot he imagined he saw the approving eye of Jehovah looking at him.

The great desk completed the décor of his office: marble walls and floors with ivory inlay, stone columns, lentils, friezes, and a great fireplace with a protruding hearthstone that had a comfortable pad for kneeling while he prayed. Next to it was a ceramic laver for his daily foot washing, an exercise he required of all the interns so they could learn obedience and humility. Sumptuous velvet curtains adorned the windows, colored a deep burgundy, and the double doors to his office were latticed in wrought iron. An intricately carved ash pole, a gift from an unknown admirer, was installed to his left. There was a 1971 Steinway Concert Grand bought by Bale at an auction, and two auditorium lobby Baccarat candelabra rested atop its closed cover. The ceiling displayed a mural of a man in the clouds, and all of it was brilliantly lit by the klieg lights recessed in the walls.

A wedding photo of Bale and his late wife Isabel sat to his right on the desk. The plump Bale, awkward in an ill-fitting, rented tuxedo had his massive arm around the tiny, hook-nosed Isabel. She was blue-eyed, red-lipped, and had pale waist-length, golden hair. In the background some girls danced gaily around a maypole.

Bale examined the sky blue French Cuffs showing from the sleeves of his white silk suit. The monograms on the cuffs peeped out at him. He straightened the black onyx cuff links, and rubbed a handkerchief on them to remove the oily prints from his fingers. When he looked into the flat dark stones he could see a gossamer reflection of his face.

How far he had come from the nights of sweaty revivals under Southern tents, where swarms of flies took shelter from the summer thunder showers while the fanning faithful sat, backlit by the lightning. The humidity was gelatinous. His cheap cotton suits, the color of dark blood from perspiration, clung to him as he gyrated between exhortation and swatting at the insects drawn to the plastic light.

"Brothers and sisters! This is a world of corruption! Of sin!"

"Amen!"

"Man is utterly depraved! He is awash in sin! You are all sinners!"

"Amen!"

"Repent!" he shouted. "Repent or be doomed to float aimlessly through the fiery pit God the Father has revealed to us!"

"Amen!"

"Are you ready? Have you gotten on your knees and begged for forgiveness? Humbled yourself before Christ, who gave himself on the cross so you could be saved? Have you thanked him for his blood?"

"Yes ! Yes!"

"Are you ready? The horn will blow and with a

mighty shout Christ will have come and gathered the faithful and you will look, and your neighbor will be gone and your wife and children will be gone and your sister and brother, and you will remain to serve the beast in a hell on earth."

"No! No!"

"There is only one way out. You must submit to authority, to the divine authority, to the authority of the church here on Earth, to the Bride of our Lord. Anything less than complete obedience means you are going to burn, and burn forever in Hell!"

"Amen!"

Starting with nothing but a Bible and an old car, Bale and Isabel traveled southern roads through a ministry of drought as humble servants of the Lord, their days of an unanchored, hardscrabble evangelism ending mostly in old motels and drafty clapboard homes. Tithing was sparse, if anything at all. Isabel passed old pie tins among the faithful for collections. Coins clattered, and a few dollar bills fluttered in the thick Southern breeze.

"We cannot do God's work without you. It is commanded that we tithe. It is commanded that we give our best to God, the first and best fruits of our labor. Ten percent is commanded. Ten percent is a minimum. Give more if in any way you can."

"You do not give God a gratuity. You do not give to Him as an afterthought. As you commit your very soul to Him so must you commit your worldly goods."

Slowly, the offerings precipitated like rivulets that ran down the top of the tent in the summer rain. As Bale's prowess as a speaker grew, those who hungered for the Word began to follow him from town to town, their mechanical donations sustaining the corpus of a ministry that found its pulse in the metallic sound of an old portable organ Isabel played when she sang hymns.

Isabel noticed that an elderly woman had been moving from town to town with the faithful. Shrunken and kyphotic, her clothes were always the same: a dark, rough cloth dress, navy blue raincoat, and marble-colored stockings that sagged. A petite, black mesh veil rested atop her chiseled winter hair.

She said nothing, reserved in her worship, and always seemed reluctant to leave the canvas temple. Isabel, who always tracked the tithing tin, saw that she never gave more than five or ten dollars. But one evening she put a note in the plate asking to speak with Bale. She remained in the last row, transfixed, until he walked back to speak with her.

"Sister, how can we help you?"

"My name is Anna Fanuel," she answered. "I am a sinner."

"So we all are, sister," Bale said. "But we are here to help the Lord save you."

"I know that brother, I sense that. I am an old woman and have spent most of my days serving the Lord in His temple. But my time is short, and you have made it clear to me that I have nothing in this world. I want to spend all of my days after this world with Him, and do not want to be apart from Him. And I must do what little I can help you spread the Word to others."

"Thank you, sister. Worldly things do not matter, only our hearts do. When you are judged, God will not count your treasure, He will look at your heart."

"I know that, and so I am giving to you today all that I have. It will leave me with nothing, as God

118

meant it to be, for I want to be with Him, and do not want to be separated from Him, just as you said. Use this to build a mighty temple for Him."

With both hands, she extended a small ash box inlaid with tiny ivory scrolling. Bale had seen no offering like it before. He opened the lid, and saw a small gold charm with a crescent moon in relief.

"What is it?" Bale asked.

"It is said to be the *saharon* worn by the prophetess at the temple where His mother first presented the Christ to the Priests after the time required for purification. Knowing Him to be the chosen one, she gave it to Him as a gift, but He let it fall from His grasp. It once had much power, and now is priceless. I ask only that it be used for His glory."

"Thank you, sister, it will. God will surely bless you. Let us pray together. 'Father, I ask for your special blessings for this woman. She has heard Your message, and has surrendered everything to You. She wants to come to You Lord, knowing that this is the only way to escape the pain of Hell. We care nothing about worldly things, but this woman knows the importance of our ministry and that we must have Your provisions to carry on Your important work. And so Lord, she comes to you in obedience, and gratitude, and asks for salvation, not the eternal separation that comes with the hellfire of damnation. Bless this woman, Lord, I pray this in Your Name, amen.' Sister, thank you so much. Go in peace. The Lord loves you."

"Bless you, Brother Bale, you have taken a burden from me," she said.

They never saw the woman again.

****

119

Bale threw the box in the trash. It looked worthless. But he did not know what to make of the amulet.

"What do you think we should do?" he asked Isabel.

"Let's have someone look at it to see if it has value. She said it was priceless, you know."

The antiquities dealer was intrigued. "I have never seen anything like this. I see many charms and amulets, and they do not impress me. But this one has, what shall I say? *Presence*, that's the word."

"What *is* it worth?" asked Isabel.

"My dear lady, do not be so hasty. These treasures can be quite powerful. Let's take a moment and admire it first. What did the person who gave it to you say?"

"I don't exactly remember, something about the Sahara."

"Hmmm. That doesn't sound quite right, but anyway, amulets like this can be most dynamic. They cure disease, protect from danger, and increase fertility. The lunular figure…"

"The what?"

"The crescent moon figure is associated with an ancient fertility goddess. The crescent of the moon, of course, resembles the horns of the bull, and we know that after the bullfight the testicles are cut off, cooked, and served to the Queen so that she…"

"See here!" Bale said, "We don't listen to pagan talk like that!"

"My deepest apologies."

"What is it worth?" Isabel insisted.

"I cannot say for certain. This will require a photo and a call to a friend. May I?" The dealer produced his phone and took several photos. "I'll be in touch."

120

A few days later while Ahab and Isabel were driving to the next revival when the cell phone rang. It was the dealer.

"You must come back at once," they heard over the crackling of the phone. "Ancient … priceless … do not leave unguarded … millions."

"What? What did you say it is worth?"

"…illions…"

****

The auditorium for the invitation-only auction in New York was filled and hushed. The amulet was featured in a glossy book that detailed its history and depicted the prophetess handing it to the Christ child while a dove descended from on high, bathed in the rays of the sun. In an appendix, dozens of letters from renowned scholars attested to its authenticity and a letter from the Internal Revenue Service noted that the proceeds from the sale would be entrusted to a tax-exempt church organization.

Bale fidgeted with his tuxedo while Isabel sipped on a glass of champagne. Stone-faced men held telephones, listened to the distant voices of faceless collectors, and prepared to whisper bids to the somber auctioneer.

"We will start the bidding at ten million dollars. Please, ladies and gentlemen, as per the published bidding rules do not make any bids in increments of less than two hundred fifty thousand dollars on this sacred object."

"…The bidding is now at ten million, seven hundred fifty thousand dollars… Am I bid eleven million dollars?"

"…Am I bid fifteen million five hundred thousand…"

"…Please, this is the rarest of objects. It would be an injustice for bidding to stop at a mere twenty-four million dollars…"

Bale wedged two plump fingers into his moist collar and tugged. Isabel mopped his brow with a cloth and swiped his few strands of hair toward the back of his head. "Really!" she hissed. "You aren't in the South anymore and we ain't going back! And stop sweating so much, and stop acting like some sort of grifter! And stop sounding like some bohunk. I swear, the first thing we are going to buy is some speech lessons for you."

"…Thank you. The bidding now stands at thirty-one million seven hundred fifty thousand…"

The gavel rapped once. "…Gentlepersons, please. Going once. Bidding is now at forty million dollars. This is hardly the time to stop giving your consideration to such an exceptional work of art that probably resided within the Holy of Holies. We are told that the Baby Jesus held it in his precious hands."

The gavel rapped again. "Going twice. I implore you, do not dishonor this consecrated tribute to our Judeo-Christian heritage. A mere forty million dollars…."

Suddenly, a new energy surged into the auditorium and lifted the bidding. "Forty-five million five hundred thousand dollars from a new bidder! A respectable increase! Am I bid fifty million dollars? Thank you, fifty million dollars."

"Thank you again, sixty million dollars, now sixty-seven, now seventy million dollars. Now, ladies and gentlemen, we are beginning to see the true worth of this magnificent talisman."

122

"Magnificent what?"

"Shhhh!" said Isabel.

"Ladies and gentlemen, eighty million dollars! The very weight and power of this antiquity can be felt in this room. It has a life of its own!"

The air conditioning was making a deep, long whumping sound and the air in the room was thick and stifling. The voice of the auctioneer was suspended over the amulet, and nothing seemed to be moving.

"Eighty-nine million dollars. Ladies and gentlemen, we cannot go on much longer … Ninety-three million now ninety-seven million dollars…" The auctioneer was fairly choking. "Ninety-eight million dollars, ninety-nine million dollars," he rasped.

"One hundred million once, one hundred million dollars twice…and three times. Congratulations to the winning bidder!" An approving murmur exhaled across the floor of the room as the air conditioner quieted and the cool air returned.

"Praise the Lord!" chortled Bale.

"We're done!" cried Isabel.

****

It did not take Isabel long to recover from the shock of success. "Well, I suppose that one hundred million will have to do… I really wanted more. But I do know one thing, Ahab, we have been chosen. I just know it. Why else would that woman have given that charm to us unless God sees something important in what we are doing? I ask you, am I right?"

"Yes, dear, of course you are right. We are the chosen."

123

Isabel decided to use the money to start an electronic ministry for God's glory. The matter was simple. A central location that had the right equipment could use television, the internet, and social media. They would build a grand digital temple of all three.

But the name, it had to have the right name. Something that would shout their fight against the corruption of the world, and God's demand for obedience, and the horrible punishment that surely follows sin. Punishment, that was the key. Isabel recalled, "And whosoever was not found written in the book of life was cast into the lake of fire." People dread punishment. Everyone is a sinner, and sinners deserve death and then punishment. It does not matter what you are, wealthy or nameless, the fear that after this life you might actually go to Hell always seethes just below the surface of peoples' lives: the awesome, subterranean fear that the Sunday pulpiteer is right; the dread that a divine gravity is pulling your guts down to some deep pit.

So Ahab and Isabel decided to call their mission the Lake of Fire Church. Fear would bring them to him. Believer and unbeliever would come to Bale for the message of salvation and immortality. Ahab and Isabel would take up the digital sword of truth.

Isabel remembered the Missouri farm where she had grown up in a family of day workers. Someday, she had vowed, it would be hers. All of it. The lush pastures, the vineyard, the lake. Isabel began buying the land around it, and when she had it surrounded she approached the grandson, a man named Nabor.

"My, how you've grown! I can remember when you were just a baby. I was a wisp of a girl then, just sixteen. And I'm so sorry to hear about your mother, she had such a hard time. I thought about her a lot, always wondering how I could help. And what a hard end she came to. But anyway, Ahab and I would like to know if you would consider selling the farm to us. You've probably heard, we want to build a great ministry for God's glory, and we want to do it right here. Our church can give you more than a fair price. We want to call it The Chariot."

"Oh, thanks, ma'am. But I don't think I want to sell. I'm the only one left, and this is the family farm. This was the promised land for us when my folks came to the States. It just wouldn't be right. I'm happy tending my own vineyard."

"Well, all right young man, we'll just have to wait and see."

A few weeks later Nabor found himself sitting before the elders at his church.

"Now see here, we can't have this!"

"Have what?"

"A sinner among us."

"What?"

"You know what we're talking about."

"What?"

"We have information that your mother sinned with a pastor's son."

"What?"

"As if you didn't know!"

"What the hell are you people talking about?"

"Your mother, sir, fornicated with the son of a former pastor of this Church. And you, sir, are the product of that sin!"

"You're crazy. My poor mother died from cancer, and my father was killed in Vietnam when I was a baby."

"Well, we have it on very good information that your mother was a whore, and that she slept with the son of an interim pastor who was here many years ago. The sins of the parents are upon the children! We have already voted. You have been disfellowshipped, and are to leave this Church."

"You can't do that! My family has belonged to this Church for generations. My great-great-grandfather helped found it. Why, I've been a deacon here. I won't stand for this!"

"It is done. You have no say, and are not welcome anymore. Leave."

Other doors in the town quickly slammed shut on Nabor. Abandoned, he had little choice but to sell to the Lake of Fire Church and move on.

"He should have sold to me when I first asked," Isabel remarked. "He would have got a better price."

****

Isabel's instinct that people craved digital and real-time anchors of structure and authority found its mark. In the early days they gave the television programs away, contented with the odd time slots on Sunday mornings. Bale's coaches trained his voice and his delivery. Isabel studied media markets. The professional sermon writers honed the messages, and Bale's powerful delivery boomed across live streaming, Facebook, and cable television.

Soon, Sunday worship at the 20,000-seat sanctuary at The Chariot channeled into a riptide of believers who, ecstatic at the procession of the 450-strong chorus called the Bale Prophets, the dance troupe, the camels, sheep, and donkeys and the simulated animal sacrifices immersed themselves into Bale's transfixing sermons.

"Sinners! You are all sinners!

"You are the fruit of a monstrous tree planted by the sin of our first father and mother and fertilized with your corruption.

"Sinners! You are stained with sin and death.

"You break God's law, the law of His Ten Commandments, not realizing that all the while you have become a part of death's plan, a plan which intends all misery ... misery in this world, and misery in the next, a misery that will consume your soul forever. And as you daily break the law He watches in horror until He can bear it no more and His almighty wrath bursts forth as unstoppable as the explosion of a sun. It is written, 'therefore shall Zion for your sake be plowed as a field, and Jerusalem shall become heaps, and the mountain of the house as the high places of the forest.'

"Sinners! Read the prophet Micah and take him into your hearts and you shall be cleansed, for God almighty hates sin.

"While you are under the guilt of sin you are under its power, and under the power of Satan. God withholds all from you, you poison yourself, and you allow Satan's laborers to pump his corruption through your veins. You wallow in sexual depravity, you kill your babies, you consume pornography, you lie, you cheat, you steal, you curse, you drink alcohol, you smoke tobacco, you use drugs, and you worship the things of this world and forsake that which is sacred.

"Sinners!

"Do you not see? Your very prosperity ruins you. You idolatrize property, you covet your neighbor's wife and his home, his car, and his success. You lust for it for yourself. You idolatrize sports, and computers, and

127

cars. And as you do so, Satan wraps you in the chains of death.

"Sinners! If you shall confess your iniquities then God will remember His covenant with you and wash them away.

"If you do not repent, then the fires of Hell await you. It is time for you to turn from evil ways and surrender to God almighty, to enslave yourself to His everlasting word. His son the Christ will soon return and will spread His wrathful judgment upon the face of the earth."

Bale's imperious messages radiated from a web-work of dishes craning at the sky and the fiber optic cable laced underneath The Chariot. The early trickle of e-mails and phone calls coagulated into a pulsing torrent of suppliants, and the cable companies soon gave substantial fees for Lake of Fire programming while vendors happily paid premium prices to run commercials personally approved by Isabel. People were captivated by "The Obedience Channel," and "The Sin Channel," and "The Salvation Channel." The call volume at the flashing LAKE OF FIRE number was handled by teams of trained operators eager to recite the message and light the way for the lost.

The Chariot's Twitter unit, the Trumpeteers, tweeted incessantly:

"Satan! Coming soon to a family near you: yours!"

"Hillary: Jezebel or Anti-Christ?"

"Old Testament Prophecy: the Bible predicted a Trump Presidency!"

"Jerusalem, the capital of Israel: One step closer to the End!"

"The Lake of Fire Church: the original millennials!"

The Lake of Fire Virtual Chapel pioneered digital worship, and the internet ministry built around it became feared and revered. At his command Bale could e-mail the millions of the faithful who had willingly given their addresses; the response rates were unmatched by any other organization. His electronic endorsement was a blessing, his denouncement, a curse. Bale's place in the Evangelical Hall of Fame was assured.

And the tithing. It was phenomenal. Bale had no explanation for the epic flood of money. The Apple Pay, PayPal and Bitcoin tithing was innovative, and widely studied. Bale's computer gave him real time numbers for the cash flow, and the ministry accountants made hourly cash sweeps. The Internal Revenue Service had looked into the church, but the phalanx of lawyers had taken care of that. The Church was free to do what it wanted.

It did not take long for the politicians to follow. Candidates for office rose and fell with an endorsement or reproach from Bale. Isabel spent hours with campaign consultants, building entire elections around Lake of Fire position papers, and an appointment with Isabel was prized by Capitol Hill lobbyists. The new airfield installed near the Chariot was a-swarm with small jets circling above.

What great glory for the Lord! There was no end in sight!

With Bale at the helm The Chariot headed for its righteous, firey apex.

****

But Satan never rested. For every success at The

Chariot there seemed to be a defeat. Bale had entered his office from his private apartment that morning and switched on the computer monitor to see his daily brief from the communications staff. The list of copycats and competitors was a bit longer every time he looked at it. There was the Church of the Apocalypse, the Fire and Brimstone Church, the Hellfire and Damnation Ministries, The Church of the New Jerusalem, the Anti- Anti-Christ Salvation Army, the New Gehenna Ministries, the Sons of Elijah, the Qumran Separatists, The Essene Remnant, The Church of the Have It All Now, and the Be'ālîm Noumenists, whoever those weirdoes were. The Internet was clotted with cyber-churches and their crypto-gods with the endless stairsteps of fees that promised, with each little payment, a better glimpse of the digital deity that would answer everything, for everyone.

But the daily brief again spent considerable time discussing the New Church of the Neo-Prophets as the gravest threat of all. Based in San Francisco, its motto, "The God in You," resonated with Americans; converts replicated by the hundreds every day. Its cyber-temples were all over the Internet and self-worship centers were sprouted across the country. The fire at the annual convention in Tucson the previous year did nothing to slow them down; hundreds had been immolated at the hand of an arsonist, and CNN showed footage of thousands of small pyres across the country lit by the prophets, who dropped photos of themselves into the flames in solidarity.

Coincidentally in the city at the time, Isabel went to the scene of destruction. "Can't these people see the wrathful hand of God?" she asked the media.

The brief also contained a summary of the attack on the Lake of Fire website. The Rainbow Rangers had run a brute force attack as a decoy while they raided the church e-coffers with a CSRF ploy at a cost of millions. Bale shifted in his chair and snorted such that his suit rippled. It didn't matter, there would be more, there was always more. He looked at the mahogany eye on the desk and a deep assurance of faith and righteousness welled in him.

He picked up the wedding photo. Isabel was gone after a brief, painful fight with cancer. She clung to life relentlessly, but the final days of unending hemorrhaging left her hospital bed soaked in blood, the sheets twisted from her thrashing. She was a godly woman, Bale thought. She would have known exactly what to do, how to take down the thieves, the perverts, the self-absorbed wackos.

But Bale was left on his own. How to respond to the satanic onslaught and defend the faith? For weeks his staff debated the issue and came up with paper after paper. It was meeting after meeting. Finally, he, Bale, stepped forward to lead them back to the Promised Land, back to the very thing that had made his ministry great. And he would preach the sermon that would allow him to secure his place among the great religious leaders of all time. Luther. Calvin. Scheeben. Edwards. Mather. Graham. Bale. History would remember him, and his enemies would go down to defeat.

He wiped his glistening head. Some thought that the klieg lights in his office were extreme; they were certainly hot to sit in. His own children refused to see him in his office, saying, "What are you trying to do? Set us on fire?" Bale liked to tell visitors that the rigorous examination and exposition of sin required intense light, but Isabel insisted on them because she feared darkness and shadows.

As he moved to loosen his collar the computer monitor flicked on: there was the crazy man, looking intently at Bale. At first Bale thought it was an errant screen shot from the security cameras, but then the eyes blinked.

"Have you found me, my enemy?" Bale asked.

The man kept looking at Bale and then, slowly, raised a tangled bunch of the black, withered grapes from the vineyard. Then he spat upon it and mouthed the words, "The sky is locked." Startled, Bale moved to turn on the audio switch so he could shout at the man.

"Reverend?"

Bale jumped in his seat, gathered himself, and said, "Come in, Micah."

"Thank you. Reverend, I know that you are busy preparing for the next worship service, but I feel like I need to speak with you about something that burdens me."

"Micah, you always bring me bad news. Be quick, the final fitting for my armor is in a few minutes.

"I'm sorry Reverend, I always try to speak from my heart."

"Then speak now."

"I am terribly concerned about Friday's sermon. I feel like God is telling me that it is a bad idea, and that we should either postpone it, or not do it at all."

"See? You always bring bad news."

"I can only tell you what I feel like the Lord says to me. You may win the day, but the result will be your destruction. Our flock will scatter."

"See? You always bring bad news to me! Did you

not sign a loyalty oath when you came to work here?"

"I did, but my first loyalty is to God."

"You are the only one here at Lake of Fire who says I should not do this. How can you be right and everyone else be wrong?"

"Perhaps God has put a lying spirit in the mouths of others."

"Nonsense! God does not do those sorts of things. Our God is the God of truth."

"I can only tell you what I believe."

"Then perhaps you should consider taking your prophecies somewhere else. They are not welcome here."

****

Thousands of the faithful filled the sanctuary, packed tightly into a single, supplicating mass. The heat radiating from their bodies stifled the air such that the women fanned themselves, trying to keep cool while the enormous air conditioning units strained under the relentless summer heat that bombarded The Chariot. The compressors, throbbing in unison, emitted a faint cardiac murmur.

The choreographed worship service had proceeded nicely. The jumbotron showed the television cameras constantly panning the crowd, and the place had the feel of a sporting event. The Bale Prophets boomed through several songs; the massive, half-acre chandelier with its 100,000 points of light above them seemed to sway in rhythm to their singing while the band kept a constant up-tempo beat.

The first pastor, a warm-up, had gone on too long, and was a bit boring. But that was all right. It left plenty of room for Bale. The *Hagag* dancers, his favorite, had just finished, and it was time for Bale to climb up onto the massive bronze chariot to lead the faithful into battle. He struggled a bit, but managed to pull his impressive girth up and in while his sword clanked at his side. A pair of anxious Lipizzaner stallions tethered to the chariot was held in check by a groomsman.

Bale drew his sword and held it on high.

"Dearest Brothers and Sisters in the Lord, like the Apostle Paul urges us I have put on the whole armor of God, the belt of truth, the breastplate of righteousness, the shield of faith, the helmet of salvation, and the sword of the Spirit so that I can deliver to you the gospel of the Lake of Fire Church.

"I am here today to tell you about a threat, a threat to our church that is so grave that our very existence in the Lord is in peril. Yes friends, this house of our dear Lord is under attack from evil itself, from Satan, from the Father of all lies, that murderer, that prince of demons who will go to any length to snatch even a single soul from salvation.

"Where, you may ask, does this attack come from? It comes from everywhere. We are besieged. Turn your attention with me to the Internet, a cyber-world that has become a hotbed of cyber-sin. In that electronic pit of Hell we see nothing but digital apostasy, digital fornication, and, I am told, programs that allow the perverts and the deviates to have digital sex with digital infants and children. O Lord! Hear my cry unto you! Bring your curses, your wrath, down upon these cyber-Sodomites! We cry out for justice!

"And this attack comes not only from the computers and the phones and tablets, but from the

pagans who are the unwitting dupes of demons and
who have surrendered themselves to the idolatries
of modern man. Too many believe that there is no
truth, that there are no absolutes, and that wanton sex,
lust, pornography, drugs, homosexuality, lesbianism,
fetishism, socialism, postmodernism, ism, ism, ism,
all of the isms that sweep across our society as part
of some fuzzy notion of a grand movement toward a
happy and just civilization where all will live in peace
and harmony; too many people believe these lies and
use them as an excuse to declare themselves as gods
when in truth they commit the sin of idolatry and
worship the false idols of themselves.

"What is at stake? Salvation. Your salvation. The
triumph over death. The lives of the innocent unborn,
of your children, your parents, your grandparents,
of everything that we believers love and cherish and
hold dear in America. Your very mortal soul is in
jeopardy. If you do not cling to God's truth you will
surely perish, condemned to an eternity as the object
of God's wrath.

"I, Bale, call upon each of you in this sanctuary,
you who watch on television, you who listen on radio,
and you who watch on streaming video to reject this,
and repent and turn back to your church, The Lake
of Fire Church, as your sole and single avenue to the
truth, to redemption, and to salvation. You must turn
away from the cyber-infamy, the cyber-idols, and the
cyber-apostasy. I command it."

He paused. Strangely, he could hear the air
conditioning, low and pulsating in the background.

"There are terrible consequences if you do not.
The consequences are death and Hell. It is written
in Deuteronomy 32:35 that 'Their foot shall slip in

135

due time.' What does this mean? It means that you who do not believe are the property of Hell. That the infinite wrath of God reserved for the unregenerate will be visited upon you, inevitably, at His pleasure, and despite your best efforts. There is nothing below your feet, nothing to keep you from falling into the gaping maw of Hell promised to the sinner. No plot or scheme of man can prevent this, for nothing can resist the will of God.

"There is no security in that you are still alive, or in good health, or that you have wealth, or family, or fame. You cannot use diligence or craft or art or your own wisdom to prevent your leaving this earth. Your schemes do not secure you from Hell. Everyone plots how he will escape damnation, and believes that his plans are unique and cannot fail. But you schemers and idolaters cannot hide from God's wrath. You are nothing but a burden upon this world; you serve sin and Satan. All the ways by which sinners leave the world are under His control. And at any time, at His pleasure, at His arbitrary and just will, you will die, despite your cunning, your planning, your conniving and scheming.

"If we could talk with those in Hell they would tell us they never planned to go there, but death came like a thief in the night, destruction came suddenly, and dashed their plans and schemes upon the rocks. And now, they cry bitterly at their folly, their vanity, their sin.

"God is dreadfully provoked, his anger is dreadfully provoked, and the Devil waits for you, held back only by the pleasure and will of God. And you who do not believe, who are not saved, who have not drawn this church around you and committed

136

your very best and first fruits to it are condemned to unending damnation, for God owes you nothing, and He will have you pitched into Hell.

"There will be no mercy, nothing will be held back, you will be thrown away and God will forget about you. You will be cast out into the abyss of eternity apart and separate from God, but not apart from His wrath. He will not pity you, but will allow the demons to trample upon you.

"How can I describe Hell? I cannot fully communicate its horrors to you because I am a mere mortal and cannot fully appreciate the terrors devised by God for those He does not know. But I do know that the God who has devised the immaculate biology of a cell and the majesty of the universe, with its billions of expressions of His beauty, has no limit to His ability to contrive torment for the wicked and the sinful. In Hell, God has compressed all of His wrath into a fury that cannot be measured with any device known to man, and in that place all sinners will be in the hands of an angry God.

"My studies have given to me a few inadequate descriptions with which I might try to inform you of the body of darkness and fire that awaits the unsaved. Let me start with something that sounds simple, yet is ghastly in its truth: Hell is the opposite of Heaven. It is an inversion of Heaven. If the happiness of heaven continues forever then so too will the misery of Hell. If the flesh is resurrected for the glories of Heaven then so too is it resurrected for the punishments of Hell, and the rewards of Heaven are matched in reverse in the tortures of Hell. Do you see? Heaven would make no sense without its opposite in Hell, and vice-versa. That is a fundamental truth of the cosmos.

137

"We also know from the Old Testament that Hell is a place of supreme darkness and disorder. It is a void, a waste, an underworld of nothingness. Our Hebrew brethren call it 'Sheol.' It is an absolute and ultimate darkness whose appetite for the living souls of the damned cannot be satisfied. Some have compared it to a great and eternal lion that feeds continuously upon living flesh, a lion the exact opposite of the beloved Lion of Judah.

"When you die you go immediately to judgment, and when judgment has been pronounced and you have been cursed for eternity, you must depart for the underworld, never to return. You cannot even look over your shoulder to see what might have been had you been an obedient Christian. The journey is long, and as you approach the gates that lead into the pit of the abyss the first flashes of heat strike you, and even though you have become a mere shadow, a shade, you nonetheless have a physical body and a sense of dread will begin to grow inside you, a dread so great and profound and unyielding that you will want to run and return to the Lord begging for forgiveness, but there is no return, there is nothing that you can do, for you have been condemned to join the billions of others who have said 'No' to obedience.

"And then the henchmen, the demons of Satan, those who are the very least of his soldiers, will gleefully grab you and thrust you through the gates of Hell and into its pit. But you will not fall some short distance before striking bottom. No, you will fall for ages and ages until you reach the pit filled with the writhing masses of the dead, a pit that has no boundaries and stretches for infinity, walled in only by the pleasure of God. And as you approach that pit in your fall the heat will become horrible and a dreadful stench, not just from yourself, but a stench from the thousands of millions of the damned who have preceded you, that stench will invade your nostrils, your lungs, your very pores so that you are completely consumed with the foul smell of Hell.

He paused, thinking, "That should get them going."

The air conditioners seemed to be making a low "whump" in unison. Where had he heard that before? Perhaps he was the only one who could hear it; no one else seemed to. But the stillness of the crowd, the looks of anguish, the tears, the cries of children told him that they belonged to him, that he had control. He must press on.

"Now, some of you may ask: 'How long does Hell last? Surely it must end sometime? Will not God someday forgive us and release us?'

"I tell you Hell does not know time. That is right. In Hell, there is no time. We have no concept of this here on Earth. Time is change, and that change is constant. Time has a beginning and an end. Only once has the sun stood still, the moon stopped, and God used that to defeat the enemies of Israel. You who have been born are nothing without a future, without time, and without space. And at some point in the future this universe will complete its unwinding and the very last quivering molecule to be found in the reaches of outer space will become cold, and the universe will die. Time will end.

"Our Lord has no past and no future. He is. We know that from His name, 'Yahweh', which means 'I am who I am.' Sunset and sunrise are of no account to Him. He sees past, present, and future all at once.

139

"And so it is with Hell. Hell does not know time, nor does the death that will consume the sinner. After millions upon millions of ages you will realize that not even a second has gone by, and that an eternity remains. You will be cast as soulless chaff upon the mighty winds that blow through Hell, lighting from place to place as the arbitrariness of Beelzebub may please.

"But Hell is also a place of fire, that great Lake of Fire from which this Church draws its name. How, you may ask, can God make a place that is both a dark pit and a lake of fire? Remember, nothing is beyond God. The eternal furnace of Hell is the product of His will. So, know also that the pit of Hell is the home of an eternal blaze, and it is the breath of God that is a stream of brimstone that is the infernal and eternal exhalation of His wrath upon you.

"And Satan, in his cunning, in his malice, in his evil, has more than a single type of fire. There is ordinary fire. It consumes. And there is the fire of fever. It burns, but does not consume. The fire of Hell burns the flesh but does not consume it. There is black fire, white fire, fire of all colors, fire that burns, and fire that freezes. Those who are cast into the lake of fire will burn in an infinitude of ways limited only by the will and creativity of God, which is infinite.

"Your body will burn, and your soul will burn. Your eyes will burn. Your fingers and your toes will shoot flames, your nostrils will inhale the cold fire of Hell, and exhale acid flames. Your sexual organs will blaze with the sins they committed while here on Earth. The twisted strands of your very DNA will sizzle until they burst into flame with the fire of the wrath of God."

He paused again, thinking, "That one will get the phones ringing."

The air conditioners were pounding now. Why didn't anyone say anything? Then he realized that the hammering was the blood in his ears, not the air conditioning. It surprised him, but he could not stop. His audience, the believers, belonged to him. He must continue.

"Sinners, beware!"

"Amen!" shouted the Bale Prophets.

"The horrors of Hell do not stop with stench and fire. No, to fully understand God's wrath upon unbelievers you must completely understand what happens to the body of the unbeliever in Hell. Although you are a mere shade, you are a shade that feels, that suffers, that agonizes. And you are in a pit filled with the countless shades of other sinners who gave offense to God, writhing together as a great mass of liquid corruption.

"Even though you try to move you cannot go very far as you struggle for even a single breath of polluted air or grovel with your mouth open for a sip of the foulest water from the acidic rain that falls upon you because you are packed in so tightly with the damned. Although maggots eat your flesh there is nothing you can do as you watch them pupate while feasting upon your body, only to become massive clouds of flesh-eating, carnivorous insects that swarm through Hell feasting upon the flesh of the damned just as locusts feast upon the crops of man.

"And the shouts, the horrible shouts of agony. The screaming. The cursing. The insults to God. Those who have lost hope, who know that they are truly dead in God's eyes let forth a single, unending cursing

141

of God that resounds as a chorus of the damned throughout Satan's kingdom.

"But do not forget that in the endless liturgy of terror in Hell you will suffer torture at the hands of demons specially chosen and trained by Satan to inflict punishment upon you. Yes, amid the swarms of insects, the shouts, the blistering heat of the inferno you will be tortured by the ingenious means devised by Satan and his minions through the eons, each more unimaginable and unspeakable than the next, and each used to show to the Lord the profound disrespect that Satan has for Him.

"Imagine for a moment the worst sufferings and torments that man inflicts upon his fellow man. Remember how the power of the atom vaporized thousands at Nagasaki and Hiroshima in an instant. Recall how the Nazis ran factories of death, how Stalin murdered millions, how Mao slaughtered the Chinese. Recall the mass graves of history, and the torment and suffering buried there with the muffled cries of the innocent. This monumental and horrible evil is nothing compared to the agonies of Hell.

"No, in Hell Satan will account for each and every soul and devise a special plan of torment just for you. Your soul will be exposed and subjected to torments beyond our feeble human imaginations. Your very substance, your breath, your spirit, your mind, your heart will all be laid bare, and burnt, ripped, shredded, chopped, mutilated, lacerated, and hammered. Unlike the human victims of Hitler and Mao and Stalin you will not have the relief of death, but instead will be dragged through endless cycles of distress under the uncaring eye of God.

"Your body, the shadow of your former self, will

likewise be tortured forever. You will be endlessly butchered, roasted, poisoned, and skewered as a pig over an open fire pit, with the delicious apple of Eve stuffed into your mouth as a hideous ornament for the insane amusement of demons as they carve you up to serve at their dinner table of evil, ripping off your chunks of roasted flesh for ghoulish consumption.

"That," he thought, "is worth at least a million dollars."

"Sinners, beware!"

The Bale Prophets shouted, "Amen!"

His preaching was so vigorous and intense he did not realize that perspiration was rolling off him onto the chariot, staining its bronze. His blood was pounding such that he had trouble hearing himself preach. He mopped his brow and continued.

"Dread diseases will invade your body and languish there. Imagine your body riddled with leprosy, swollen to the point of bursting. Open sores fester upon your skin, and your eyes, and your mouth, and your organs. The Aids virus pumps through your veins, clotting your arteries and seizing the flow of blood. Satanic microbes grow and congeal together to fill your lungs so you cannot breathe, and acid toxins secrete from your body in places I cannot mention because of the women and children.

"And in Hell there are no doctors other than demons learned in the medieval arts of medicine: leeches, toxins, acid poultices and incantations designed to punish, not cure.

"You will be bled. And as the henchmen of Satan open wounds to bleed you at their evil pleasure your once-precious fluids will gush out in an unending swirl of viscous, bloody liquid that will accumulate with the

143

serum of the other damned, and you will slowly, slowly, amid a stream that does not know time, find yourself drowning in an endless lake of blood that rises up and invades your open mouth, your nose, your lungs, your belly, your eyes, your ears, your pores, and permeates the very core of your eternal senses until you gurgle and choke upon the entire sin of the cosmos that has congealed into the perversion of the underworld. And all the while, Satan's stooges will dance around you, gleefully slashing themselves into a bloody frenzy, their own toxic fluids mingling with yours and that of the other damned."

"Oh ho," he thought, "my enemies turn back, they stumble and perish before you." He looked at his watch, noting the time. "I need to be sure and check and see if the tithing jumped when I said that."

"Sinners, beware!"

"Amen!" the Bale Prophets shouted on cue.

"But we have not considered the soul. What happens to the soul in Hell? You have a soul, but we actually know very little about the soul and many preachers never discuss it because they do not know what to say or how to describe it. So let me offer to you a way to think about your soul. Think of it as a pair of gossamer lungs made of the lightest, most delicate substance known to God or man, a substance like something that you might see floating in the air on a calm, beautiful summer day, and it is filled with the energy of God and the brilliant, pure light of God so that it is a beacon that shines inside you. It is what makes you in His image. Now imagine the exact opposite of that, that those same lustrous vessels that breathe the divine grace in and out have been dissected and pinned to a board, flayed open just like

144

an insect or a frog that you might find on display in a biology classroom, and the light of your wondrous essence has pulsed slower and slower until it has gone out and has now been abused and profaned so that what would have been exalted in heaven is now fully debased into a blackened shroud of breathless depravity. Satan and his minions urinate and defecate upon it. That is what happens to your soul in Hell."

His nose felt wet: he dabbed at it with the handkerchief, and the bright red blood on it surprised him. His blood still pounded in his ears and he felt a sharp pain in his side, as if he had been wounded by an arrow or a shot, and he cringed. But Bale gathered himself and continued.

"Death stalks us all. And just as the Bible predicts, the end of days closes in about us; evil is on a rampage and this evil order must be brought to a close. Do you not see? The Bible tells it all, if only you know how read the secret codes and make the hidden calculations. The Bible will tell you all if you know how to read it.

"It is written in Daniel 8:14. 'unto 2,300 days, then shall the sanctuary be cleansed, or justified,' and in Daniel 9:24 it says 'seventy weeks are determined upon thy people to make an end of sins.' God has spoken to me and has shown me the true meaning of Daniel, the secret calculations of when Christ shall come again, and I have made those calculations given to us in Daniel and I am here today to tell you that the return of Christ is upon us! Is going to happen now! His reign of 1000 years will start at any moment, so sinners beware! The terrible threshing of the tribulations is about to start where the wheat will be separated from the chaff and the unbeliever will be thrown into Hell!

145

And it is only the true believers who will survive and become the priests and kings of heaven.

"My staff and I have created a special algorithm derived from secret Bible codes to identify the 144,000 elected for salvation and to form the new church; you who sit here today are among them, you are the Army of the Elect chosen by Christ to declare war upon the darkness and to throw Satan and the damned into the pit. It is we who are the direct descendants of Israel, it is we who are the descendants of the lost tribes of Israel, and it is we who have been chosen with our British brothers and sisters to lead Christ's kingdom on Earth. We shall rise up and seize this moment, and, if need be, we shall take to the streets to cut down our enemies and the enemies of Christ who would thwart His return. It is our God-given responsibility to moralize a fallen world through the use of force."

Bale thrust his sword upward into the lights.

"And for this battle I have for each of you a sword. The sword of truth and the sword of the spirit. And as you receive that sword you must declare your complete and total obedience to God, and to me, Bale. Do so or you are lost, condemned to Hell with the other sinners. It is I, Bale who will lead you, I, Bale, who will...."

There he was! The man in the cameras, the man who had eluded him; there he was in the gallery staring at Bale in the same deep, scornful way. Bale moved to speak and have security grab the man and detain him, but his tongue was thickened and his throat numbed. The pain shot through his side again and he doubled over. Bale grabbed the chariot and pulled himself up to see the man looking up at the ceiling and pointing at the chandelier.

The chandelier came loose and dropped on the

Bale Prophets, crushing them. The heaped points of light blinked in a chaotic unity as the congregation gasped, followed by screams of alarm and anguish. The jumbotron closed in on Bale's face so that it filled the entire screen: his eyes bulged to the extreme and blood streamed from his nose. The sweat rolled off of him and his mouth hung open as if paralyzed. An unseen finger drew a line across his heart, opening the aorta as cleanly as a surgeon's scalpel, and his body arched backward magnificently, as a bow does when the string is drawn back slowly. Then, as if an invisible hand had placed itself on the back of his head, he snapped forward and his face smashed onto the podium. Bale's blood gushed out onto the pulpit and down onto the chariot floor. He collapsed, his body shivering hideously, his armor clanging against the bronze walls. The sanctuary was quiet for a moment, and then panic seized the place.

Outside, a small, fist-sized cloud appeared on the horizon. Soon, the clouds balled up and it began to rain. Fouled with Bale's blood the chariot was rolled outside, where it was hosed down. There the wolves gathered, lapping up the water.

Restoration House
Where Misery Loves Company®

The Stone-Campbell Association of Companies,
Proprietors

But I discipline my body and keep it under control....

1 Corinthians 9:27 (ESV)

Crackling across the rattling speaker of an old brown Motorola radio, the amplitude-modulated voice of Tennessee Ernie Ford was singing:

> You load sixteen tons, what do you get?
> Another day older and deeper in debt.
> Saint Peter, don't you call me, 'cause I can't go....

Three bluish-gray beehive coiffures bobbed in unison to the ol' pea-picker, right-left, left-right, right-left. The ladies were seated side-by-side on a Naugahyde sofa, their pasty plumpness evident in their taut, monochromatic McCall pattern dresses that strained and buckled as they undulated with the pulsing of the radio's coarse brown cloth cover, and the dim vacuum tubes inside.

> "I owe my soul to the company store........."

Ford's plaintive baritone lingered to an end, was followed by morbid woodwinds, and the three heads paused together as the song finished. The somber voice of the radio DJ intoned, "and that, sinners, ends another session of 'Jammin' with Job,' here on radio station WHFB, The Big Burn."

The three sighed together. "Oh, I just love that song," one said.

"That Ernie Ford knew how to suffer," said another.

"Even if it was inside a bottle," said the third, and the three tittered like naughty schoolgirls.

The ladies were longtime residents at Restoration House, a large, plain red brick affair whose two stories covered an entire city block. The building had seen a succession of uses during its life, first as a slaughterhouse, then as a cold storage facility, and then as a distribution center for a commode manufacturer. Its present incarnation as an assisted living home for elderly members of the One True Church had come about during an unusual period of close fellowship among a group of believers whom fate had somehow mashed together following a catastrophic national election that had seen the Democrats sweep the White House and both Houses of Congress. Dozens of senior citizens of an apocalyptic sort of disposition spontaneously gathered in a football stadium where the giant floodlights had been left on, and in a fit of unity in the Spirit and the deep conviction of the Sin of self and others it was agreed that the End of Days was surely at hand, and that a holy huddle of believers was the best defense to the tribulations soon to come.

An especially repentant and financially successful member of this independent new church who owned the large building in question kicked out the commode manufacturer, donated the property to a brand new 501(c)(3) limited liability company that, for propriety's sake, was operated under the assumed name of an association, and began the extensive renovations necessary to turn the property into a fortress against the onslaught of the democratic vices of the new millennium.

The vision was that the elderly faithful would reside with some assurance of peace and (perhaps) salvation in an assisted living facility that would care for them as they made the transition from this world to the next in the chaotic seas of uncertain times. To that end the building was reinforced with No. 1 steel ("There's Always a Solution in Steel"), encased in a double-wall of custom blood-red fire brick, and in a reckless moment of concession to the building authorities, was provided with a few begrudging windows that more properly resembled the sort of slits found on armored bank vehicles and juvenile detention centers. A pair of certified fire doors at the front opened into a vestibule of sorts that in turn led down a straight and narrow passage to a secure door with a custom Maglock® opened only by an adjacent biometric fingerprint scanner or a fully-encrypted, hack-proof Clapper® with rolling algorithmic Bible codes specific to the church member.

That door opened into a vast two-story fellowship hall where the life of the community took place. What struck one's eye immediately were the unadorned walls painted a stark off-white and amplified by thousands of fluorescent lights that gave the place the effect of being inside a very large refrigerator with the door continuously open. The single men's dormitory rooms were stationed to the east and the women's to the west; married couples resided in a series of apartments in a capacious overhead loft. At the north end of the building was the dais for singing and preaching, the baptistery was raised behind it, and a cafeteria had been built onto the west side.

The primitive simplicity of the place belied its purpose: that life should be lived in the same way as the earliest of the believers and that sin should be exposed in the raw, both of which explained the persistent busyness of the place: the demands of fellowship and the tireless monitoring of the sin of others called for the extremes of the discipline of vigilance.

The bustle and din was kept in motion by a parrot that constantly screeched the only two phrases its owner, a stern little widow woman, Mrs. Bunion, who had led women's Sunday school for decades without fail, had taught it: "Their foot shall slide in due time!" and "Thus saith the Lord!"

And although the sin of the world was kept on the outside, no less attention was paid to the sin inside Restoration House. A Texas software engineer equally terrified at the wholesale collapse of America turned up at Restoration House and offered his unique services to its Elders. The man had overseen an apartment project at UT Arlington for senior citizens designed to promote independence and clean living. The flooring there was studded with thousands of sensors and could detect the slightest movements of the smallest muscles in the human body. Cameras tracked skin color for indications of disease, and mirrors registered pulse and blood pressure. The sheets and pillowcases detected movement and breathing.

Some simple changes in the computer coding gave birth to a new program, fondly nicknamed "Sin-O-Matic," that was tirelessly overseen by Mrs. Bunion in a sealed room, and who, so far as anyone knew, never slept. As she sat in the room crowded with computers and monitors and sensors, the severe hair bun on the top of her head was backlit by computer monitors, and the parrot made for a silhouette on her shoulder.

The rooms at Restoration House could detect the slightest changes in limbic activity, excessive heart rates, blood pressure and respiration, and the sensors in the sheets analyzed telltale bodily fluids. The pillowcases could read unusual head movements, the mattresses tracked jerking motions, and at nighttime the floor sensors could detect any suspiciously high incidence of footsteps upon which the lights snapped on, followed by a brisk rapping at the door that told of Mrs. Bunion. Underwear with cutting edge nano-technology was being developed to detect the overstimulated and the sated.

On this particular day Restoration House was unusually quiet because its denizens languished in the satisfied exhaustion of exuberance, as they were fatigued by the aftereffects of excessive righteousness. The previous week had been the annual Jubilee Revival, and the days and nights abounded with activities. Works shops during daylight hours considered vital topics such as:

You're suffering: Is it Enough?

Thank God! (I'm not a Baptist)

The Pope: Anti-Christ or Spawn of Satan?

Apostates Anonymous
(Roll Call at 10:00 a.m.)

Easy Steps to More Effective Misery

Guns and God: What Would Jesus Pack?

Can't Miss Signs of the End of Days

In the evenings the grand hall was cleared and rows upon rows of chairs were set out for the preaching, and the most famous of the voices of the Gospel had come through: Brothers Jimmy "Lockjaw" Jones, Barton Campbell, Ira "Fiery Irey" North, Alexander Stone, E.H. Ijams, John Dee Cox, Larry "Cyclone" Smothers, and Davis "Windbag"

McClellan. Each had enthusiastically moved the faithful along the ridgeline of life, with Heaven on one side and Hell the other.

"There is only one true church of Christ," began Cyclone Smothers. "The church that began in the year 33 when a mighty roar came down from the heavens and the winds of God filled the room where the Christians hid fearing for their lives, the winds that shook that house to its timbers, and the winds that shook this sinful world for all of time until the return of Jesus Christ to sit in judgment of the evil, and the wicked, and those who are not of the One True Church!"

"Thus saith the Lord!" screeched the parrot.

"The world, the truth, your life is black and white, the black and white of the letters on the pages of the Bible. There is no truth other than the truth in the pages of the King James Bible, and there is no true church other than the church as we know it in the New Testament of the King James Bible. All other truths are false … all other churches are false … and any other claims to truth and the Bible and the church are the works of the Devil!

"And who is the enemy of the One True Church? The Devil! Satan! He is the father of all lies and he lurks everywhere, even in the pages of Bible translations that distort the word of God. That's right, the NIV, the ESV, the NASB, are all works of Satan, all false translations, all with false paths to salvation…. and all filled with the sin of the world."

The mood in the room chilled.

"And each of you has the evil seed which forms into the root, the taproot, of sin. It is written, people, in Ezekiel 18:2, the soul that sins shall die."

155

"Their foot shall slide in due time!" screamed the parrot.

"So be ever on your guard, be watchful, look over your shoulder, look at your neighbor, when you go to your room today look in the mirror at yourself and see your sin for what it is.

"You can never rest, never have peace until after you stand at the judgment throne and have heard, 'Well done, faithful servant.' Because until that time God watches you, judges you, puts you on His terrible scales and weighs your sin against your works."

The skills of these righteous voices of the kingdom carried the denizens of Restoration House to the lofty heights of salvation and then swept them so deeply into the depths of damnation that the collective, but happy, despair of the believers filtered through the entire building and strained the heating and cooling system. Even Mrs. Bunion's parrot was exhausted, and although its watchful eyes were always open, the poor animal was nonetheless deep asleep.

The culmination of the Jubilee Revival had been the evening before, when Brother J.G. Malphurs made a surprise appearance and personally conducted a session of his famous Bible School Bowl, the adult entertainment favorite. Malphurs had concocted a special set of questions just for his friends at Restoration House, and the effect had been explosive.

Malphurs selected four residents and sat them at a table where each had a buzzer in front of them. As Malphurs asked the questions, the contestant who knew the answer smacked the buzzer and was called on to answer, with the exception of one poor cockeyed fellow who kept missing.

"First question!" cried Malphurs. "Satan and his

minions are chasing you. Should you:
  a) Throw a Catholic at them and get away in the confusion?
  b) Put on the whole armor of God and battle them to the death?
  c) Give them the address for the Southern Baptist Convention?
  d) Shout them straight to Hell!"

The audience called out answers, with (c) the favorite, when a quick little woman whose skin was stretched so tautly over her frame that it gave the appearance of the faded head of a bongo drum, popped the buzzer and yelled, "Shout them straight to Hell!"

"Correct!" Malphurs said. "Next question!

"Two Mormons corner you in a gas station and start telling you about the angel Moroni and the Book of Mormon. Should you:
  a) Douse them with gasoline and set fire to them?
  b) Let the air out of their bicycle tires and run away?
  c) Choke them with their neckties and take their backpacks?
  d) Shout them straight to Hell?"

The crowd started yelling answers again, and two of the contestants had guessed wrong when the quick little woman hit the buzzer again: "Shout them straight to Hell!"

"That's right!" Malphurs cried.

Soon the players were hitting the buzzers in a broken staccato while the audience, caught up in the game, started crying out in unison after every question.

"A Jew asks your daughter out on a date."

"Shout them straight to Hell!"

"Your daughter wants to marry a Buddhist."

"Shout them straight to Hell!"

"Your son wants to join a rock and roll band."

"Shout them straight to Hell!"

"A Quaker invites you to a prayer meeting."

"Shout them straight to Hell!"

"Your wife tells you she is gay and is leaving you."

"Shout them straight to Hell!"

"Some Muslims have applied for a permit to build a mosque in your community."

"Shout them straight to Hell!"

The parrot, a new phrase imprinted upon its tiny avian brain, began squawking, "Shout them straight to Hell!" with the residents, and even the calloused Mrs. Bunion managed a slightly twisted smile. And so the game went on until the 9 p.m. bedtime bell rang and the exhausted, but united and happy group trundled off to bed.

Now Satan feared the good people and the good works of Restoration House, and he took notice and began to spread the seeds of dissension. What at first seemed to be an honest dispute over tithing soon erupted into a schism that shook the steel girders of the place.

"Gross!"

"No, it's adjusted gross!"

"Gross income, the Bible says you tithe ten percent of your gross income!"

"No it doesn't. Anyone with any sense, anyone but you, you fool, would understand it has to be ten percent of net income! Render unto Caesar what is Caesar's means the government gets its cut off the top. Then you tithe on what is left."

"The Jews didn't do it that way. You don't read anywhere in the Bible that they gave the tax collectors a cut before they tithed. First and best fruits, start to last. That means ten percent off the top."

And to the delight of the Devil the schism quickly parted into a Red Sea of division accented by a steady "chunk, chunk, chunk," early on a Monday morning. The residents of Restoration House looked at the common area and saw Mr. Mortimer, a gnomish man with extraordinarily broad shoulders and a spine severely hunched by time and labor, carrying hod back and forth with the efficiency of a dung beetle. He had an impossibly narrow waist and a bald head with no neck, which gave him something of the appearance of an aging hooded cobra in dungarees. Mortimer seemed to exhale plumes of mortar dust as he chunked cinder blocks into the middle of the floor, and he quickly began to erect a wall straight down the middle of Restoration House.

As the retired mason worked, it did not take long for the folks prone to schism to figure out what was up. The ensuing shuffle, trading of rooms and bargaining resulted in a cross-migration between the gross and adjusted gross camps. Mortimer, whose indefatigability led some to speculate that he was kin to Mrs. Bunion, worked tirelessly until the wall was completed and stretched the entirety of the great area up to the worship area, which was left open since the preacher, despite his godliness, could not be in two places at

159

once. A retired sheetrock tradesman finished the wall and volunteers painted it, curiously, black on one side and white on the other.

Being ever vigilant about (the other fellow's) sin, some residents felt it only proper to drill a few clandestine holes to make certain that nothing untoward and beyond the reach of Mrs. Bunion's technologies was taking place on the other side. However, the limitations of this surveillance soon became apparent when it was discovered that damned little could be seen through holes in cinder block, and that a broomstick in the eye was unpleasant in the extreme.

Tensions peaked, however, when two fellows in the adjusted gross camp decided to take up the accordion and the banjo. A more hellish combination could not be imagined by the gross income camp, who took it as a personal affront to the sacred tradition of *a cappella* singing at Restoration House. That led the gross income residents to form a choir, and the increasing volume of competing noise on the two sides resembled the call and response caterwauling of a tomcat clinic, and led to repeated visits from the authorities following bitter noise complaints from the residents at a nearby recovery house.

At breakfast one morning the eagle-eyed denizens of Restoration House could not help but take notice of a new person sitting off by himself. He was quite tall, but reed-thin and angulated in bearing. He sported a pork-pie hat, which drew commentary about poor manners, a Vandyke, and tortoise shell glasses with thick lenses that made his eyes look as if they swam in a fishbowl. Completing the effect were black skinny jeans with a belt so small that it had to come from the

children's section in a department store, a neat brown
and green plaid sport coat with crisp, thin lapels, and
a small brown leather briefcase stuffed with papers.
His outfit never varied, and when he moved about
Restoration House it was with a mingled shamble,
caused in part by the tendency of his knees to point
outward in opposite directions.

The widowed and single women immediately
homed in upon the hapless fellow as he tried to
introduce himself.

"My name is E.A. Sous," he said.

"Is that French?" asked one of the troupe. "I don't
think I have ever met a Frenchman."

"Are you married, divorced? Ever been married or
divorced?"

"Er, no," Sous replied.

"Well," exhaled a jubilant widow, "how *do* you do!"

"How did such a nice man like yourself wind up
here?" asked another.

"I'm Mrs. Bunion's nephew," Sous said, and a
shudder rippled across the group; but the chill brought
on by the mention of Mrs. Bunion's name quickly
dissipated and they continued on. "I actually only met
her just now," Sous mentioned, "I've spent most of
my life overseas doing mission work. I won't be staying
here for very long."

The latter statement brought about a mixed
response among the women of Restoration House:
some deflated on the spot and sagged off, while
others determined to redouble their efforts at making
themselves known to this intriguing man. The intensity
of the examination made Sous uncomfortable in the
extreme. He retreated to his room where he came
under the nano-tech scrutiny of his aunt, but whose

various monitors were unable to detect anything unbiblical, and, indeed, little of anything whatsoever.

Sous's presence seemed to have a calming effect on Restoration House. The food tasted fresher, the plants looked sprightly, and the water hinted at the taste of grapes. The members' ailments, always a lively topic of discussion and competition, went on vacation and left the residents facile and generous in spirit. The house cat which, to the delight of the parrot, incessantly hacked up hairballs, suddenly found its stomach calmed. Sous moved easily among both camps, and became a popular seat at the cafeteria table.

Satan took notice of this distasteful turn of events and could not let the matter stand. He dispatched his minions, who roosted in the beams of the former commode factory and began picking at the residents until they realized there was some unsettled schismatic business to attend to. The tithing factions regrouped and quickly began competing for Sous's allegiance. The man was soon awash in biblical quotations, solicitations, exhortations, protestations, remonstrations, bromides, threats, and general politicking. Sous tried to take the high road.

"We are told to love our enemies. Perhaps prayer would help us through this difficulty," he said.

Someone answered, "I thought it was the other way around. Love your neighbor and hate your enemy."

"No, I am certain that rule was changed," Sous replied. "Perhaps prayer…."

"Some things are past prayer, Sous," a portly man said. "The curtain here is torn in two."

Sous flinched. "This place is in reverse," he

162

thought.

Despite Sous's best efforts the situation deteriorated further. The divisions grew more deep, and the tithing arguments more arcane. Two of the members went at it.

"Deuteronomy 14:22: 'year by year you shall set aside a tithe.' The Bible says nothing about adjusting for any taxes the kings commanded. The Jews were commanded to give ten percent of everything, no exceptions."

"Oh? The Jews never heard of the Internal Revenue Service. It commands that we pay taxes. Romans 13:1, 'There is no authority but by act of God, and the existing authorities are instituted by him.' God put the IRS in place, it gets its cut off the top, and saying otherwise is to defy it and be in sin."

"Well I, for one, intend to tithe from my gross income. Malachi 3:10: 'Bring the tithes into the treasury, all of them; let there be food in my house. Put me to the proof, says the LORD of Hosts, and see if I do not open windows in the sky and pour a blessing on you as long as there is need.' I put Him to the test, and He will pour his riches down upon me. He owes me."

"You're a mercenary of grace! He doesn't care about whether we tithe from the gross or adjusted gross. He...."

"Perhaps," Sous interjected, "He cares about our hearts, and ...."

"Butt out!" the two residents cried simultaneously, and they turned together to lash out at Sous, who was taking a step backward when an excited woman ran into the room.

"It's Mrs. Bunion! Mrs. Bunion! She's passed out cold on the floor!"

Sous tilted toward the stairs, broke into a jaunt and angulated up the steps four at a time. When he reached the room he found Mrs. Bunion lying on the flat of her back on the floor. She was a ghastly blue color, the right side of her face was slouched, and a wisp of spittle leaked from the side of her mouth. Sous heard the desperation of a death rattle, and he saw her helplessness and fear.

"Auntie, Auntie," he whispered to her. "It is not your time, Auntie. You have work to do." He lay his hands upon her, closed his eyes, and breathed deeply. By now a small crowd had gathered in the room, but Sous was impervious to them. He had remained rock-still for several moments when Mrs. Bunion's eyelids fluttered, and looking up at Sous she said, "Elisha, is that you?" Those were the last words she ever spoke.

"Yes, Auntie, it's me," he said softly. "Now let's get you into bed where you can rest." Downstairs the parrot started shrieking madly, "Thus saith the Lord! Thus saith the Lord! Thus saith the Lord!"

"Silence," Sous said quietly, and the parrot, struck dumb, wriggled mightily on its perch and craned its neck to the full as it kept trying to bray, but to no avail.

The episode unnerved the entirety of Restoration House. The house bard and sometime theologian, Uncle Isaac, expounded upon the matter as he sat on a stool in a corner and washed down good old American hot dogs with good old American Coca-Cola.

"Now we know as a matter of scriptural truth that the miraculous powers stopped in the first century A Dee. And what we saw here was something not of this world. So good ol' logic and rationality tells us that if the miraculous powers no longer exist and what we saw was not of this world then what we saw was something evil. And I don't need to say who or what I am talking about."

The comment flashed through the dry tinder of Restoration House, and the fires of the fear of the demonic crackled among its residents. Sous, who could be deathly obtuse at times, took no notice of the hard stares, snorts, or sneers, or the fact that he was suddenly dining alone. His habit, anyway, was to spend most of the day in his room, and Mrs. Bunion's successor at the Sin-O-Matic quickly noticed and informed everyone that the cutting-edge monitoring equipment detected absolutely nothing.

"That ain't no human bean," Uncle Isaac said.

The Father of all Lies took pleasure in this unexpected turn of events and decided to let matters move forward on their own. And, if he were fortunate, history might repeat itself, for he knew that Sous had by lot drawn the preaching slot for the next Wednesday evening church service. In keeping with good Restoration tradition godly men were called to preach, and at Restoration House the call was left to the guiding hand of the Holy Spirit as exercised through the casting of lots, and Sous's number, as it were, came up.

To say that the Wednesday morning atmosphere at Restoration House was grave would be to understate the matter, for the air had the quality of brimstone that had been smoldering for several centuries without ventilation. The parrot, which had since regained its tongue, was screaming incessantly, repeating "Their foot shall slide in due time!" and "Shout them straight to Hell!" in various pitches and inflections that were both new and alarming in the extreme, and stuffing the animal into a cage and pulling a sheet over it had no effect.

165

Even Sous took notice of the dismal quality of the place, but it never occurred to him that the pervasive morosity had anything to do with the widespread conviction that he was some sort of a demon that had penetrated the otherwise secure defenses of the fellowship.

After an opening prayer Sous stepped up onto the dais and took his seat upon a stool. Somehow, he managed to sit cross-legged with his Bible in his lap, and holding his arms out to the bristling brethren he began, "My brothers and sisters, I want to speak to you tonight about the kingdom of God. We all know that Christ preached that we must repent, for the kingdom of God is upon us. And we all believe that someday Christ will return and that he will begin his reign over a true kingdom here on Earth that will last forever."

There were a few harrumphs, but Sous had said nothing anyone could really disagree with. Still, the room had a pregnant hostility to it, and many of the House members found themselves leaning forward on their seats as if poised to lunge.

"But tonight I want to spend a few moments with you in the book of Luke. How many of us have ever thought about Luke 17:20-21 where it is written, 'The kingdom of God cometh not with observation: Neither shall they say, Lo here! or, lo there! for, behold, the kingdom of God is within you?'"

The eyes of the group narrowed uniformly, for the scent of heresy was now in the air.

"Some versions of the Bible translate Luke 17 as saying the kingdom of God is among you or in the midst of you, not within you, but I like "within" better because it speaks to how the kingdom is in our hearts and our spirits, right here and right now, and it is talking not just about each of you but of all of us, the kingdom of God is in all of us. That means you don't have to wait, the kingdom of God is right here, right now; it's in your heart."

"Liar!" someone shouted.

"That's not what that means!" shouted someone else.

"That means it was Jesus who was there and is the Kingdom," came another shout.

"No it doesn't! It means that it's so close that you can touch it but you can't touch it because you can't get it while you're here, you have to pass judgment, and it means you'd better be good or you'll burn!" came another shout.

"Brothers and sisters, no, all I am trying to say is that perhaps the second coming has already happened, and that Christ and His kingdom are in your hearts right here, right now...."

That went through the room like a shot, and the crowd launched a volley of black rectangles at Sous, who, in his usual imperviousness failed to take heed of the near misses, the arthritic aim of the members of Restoration House being the only thing that kept him from getting it straight in the head, until someone got lucky and placed a shot square in his chest. Jolted, Sous looked down and saw that the little black book was open to the title page of a copy of Nelson's "Soul Winners' Checkbook Edition" of the New King James version of the New Testament.

By then the crowd had switched to whatever was at hand and began heaving the leftovers from dinner until an overripe tomato caught Sous in the face and knocked his glasses off. As he looked down he saw the red juice and the seeds drip onto the pages of his Bible, and in that moment his peril snapped into focus.

Someone rapped a cane sharply on the floor and shouted, "Blood of Christ, Blood of Christ!" and continued to rap his cane while chanting. The others quickly joined in with their walkers and their sneakers, stamping while yelling, "Blood of Christ! Blood of Christ!" until the place was a chorus of calls for gore. Mrs. Bunion, sitting in a wheelchair with her eyes ablaze, tried to speak up for Sous, but could not.

Seeing the situation for what is was, Sous thought,

"once is plenty for me," just as another copy of the soul winner's checklist caught him upside the head and knocked his hat off.

Sous momentarily lost himself and shouted, "You shut the kingdom of heaven against men, for you neither enter yourselves, nor allow those who would enter to go in!" which served only to incite the crowd even more.

Because the House members had begun to crab their way to the dais Sous had to act quickly. He grabbed his hat and straightened his tie, lunged past the tremulous assault line to his briefcase on the front row, and after snatching it, juked and spun his way past the few people between him and the door, and made his exit.

The crowd spilled out after him shouting, but all they could see was Sous running at full speed, his knees askew with papers leaking behind him from his briefcase while the parrot cried anew, "The Kingdom of God was among you! The Kingdom of God was among you!"

The Full Immersion Baptist Church

"Brother Ass"
-Sobriquet of St. Francis of Assisi for his body

Go ye into all the world, and preach the gospel to
every creature. He that believeth and is baptized shall
be saved; but he that believeth not shall be damned.
And these signs shall follow them that believe; In my
name shall they cast out devils; they shall speak with
new tongues; They shall take up serpents; and if they
drink any deadly thing, it shall not hurt them; they
shall lay hands on the sick, and they shall recover.

Mark16:15-18 (KJV)

"Hit don' cownt!"

"Hit dew teuw!"

"No hit don't!" hissed the Church member.

"Yew don' haf tuh git the hole feller unner the wawter for hit to cownt," snapped the other member.

"Dew teuw!"

The small Baptist Church nestled in Appalachia was a good distance from the nearest highway. The faithful had to park their cars on a gravel road and walk up a steep, narrow path to the clapboard building that had once been a schoolhouse. On Sundays, the elderly and infirm had to be carried, or pulled backwards up the hill in wheelchairs.

The single room was perfectly square in height and width, thanks to the keen eye of a carpenter from a time long forgotten. The Church members carefully maintained the building, packing materials and supplies up the hill during good weather. Standing outside, they would admire the clean lines and perfect symmetry of the steeple. When the weather turned bad the path became slippery, and it wasn't unusual for someone to get hurt from a fall or a trip.

Once, when the time came to replace the windows, a man brought a pack mule that carried the new casings on either side. The mule, reluctant because of the difficult grade and the loose footing, had to be beaten on its hindquarters with a rod to encourage it upward. After the fourth trip the mule decided that it had given enough service to the Lord for the day, and quit.

Undeterred, a few members began simultaneously striking the poor animal on its haunches which did prod it, albeit haltingly, back up the hill. However, even mules reach their limit and it gave up near the crest, lost its balance, and went rolling down the hill, braying loudly. The windows were smashed to pieces, as were the faithful who wielded the rods and had the misfortune to get caught up with the beast. They too went down the hill in a moving heap of splayed arms and legs, shouts of helpless surprise, and cloven hooves.

The gritty persistence of the chosen, however, yielded much fruit. The building was so tightly sealed off from the world that at Sunday worship the air did not move. Although the building had a wood stove it had no electricity for air conditioning, so that regardless of the season the sanctuary had the thickness of hothouse air. Nothing, even time, seemed to penetrate it. When Sunday worship concluded and the doors opened, the air from outside rushed inward with the sound a soda can makes when its seal is broken.

The present controversy arose when Jedidiah Jones determined that he needed to be baptized. Advanced in years, Jones knew his days were drawing to a close. He desired to make his peace with his Lord, and asked to be baptized at his mother's church up on the hill.

Trouble was, Jones's body had been paralyzed from the neck down since a fall many years ago. He had no control whatsoever over his bodily functions, and the years of muscle atrophy had contorted his arms and legs into an angulated ball. The baptistery at the church was not deep enough to fully submerse him for a proper baptism. No matter how they rolled him some part of his body stuck up out of the water: a hand, a knee, a twisted foot. Left fatigued and sputtering, they had to stop administration of the sacrament to Jones for fear of drowning the man, and until they could figure out what to do.

The full immersionists shouted down the scriptural laxities of the other members and informed Jedidiah that complete immersion was necessary for the baptism to be any good. But because they could not fit him into the church's pool, and winter made baptism in the river impossible, he would have to go elsewhere.

"Ah ain' gittin' beptaized nowheres but tchere!," he shouted at the members.

Their alarm grew. A soul was at stake, and eternity left no margin for error. A baptism not done properly was no baptism at all, and no baptism meant no salvation, and that meant damnation.

The deacons sent the matter to the trustees, who sent the matter to the building maintenance committee. The carpenters patiently studied the plan, mindful that any additions to the baptistery had to match exactly the perfections of the building. They concluded it would be necessary to tear out the sides, hammer the concrete floor, dig several feet into the ground (while hoping and praying they did not hit rock), pour a new base, build the walls, reset the plumbing, and install a molded tub. Since they were making a major change to the building they might as well order a custom fiberglass baptistery tub for durability.

A project this size had to be budgeted, which meant the matter had to go back to the trustees. Once they had estimates, the trustees sent the matter to the deacons, who quickly determined that funds would have to be raised. That meant special sermons on tithing, bake sales, car washes, and whatever else could be done to raise money. And just getting the custom fiberglass tub up to the church was a problem in itself. No pack mule could carry the thing, and a team of mules could not drag it up the steep hill on a sled. Would they have to hire out a helicopter? Lord, how much would that cost? What about taking out a loan to speed things up? No, borrowing money wasn't biblical, so that would not do. Besides, no one was willing to sign for the loan.

No matter, a man's salvation was at stake. The renovations must proceed apace. The entire church threw itself into the project. The women began planning the bake sales, the preacher began writing the sermons on selfless giving, and the men began to tear at the foundations of the building.

On a Saturday morning the place was a beehive. The front doors were thrown open and men were tearing out the guts of the building; pieces of broken timber, pipe, and twisted metal were hauled out and thrown into a heap. The sounds of hammer against metal had the odd clanging of a rusted church bell.

A young boy came running up the hill and into the sanctuary. The men took no notice of him as he bent over, gasping to catch his breath. Finally, he straightened up and tried to get their attention. Not succeeding, he spoke out, "Haiy!" No one responded.

"Haiy, ah sed!" Nothing still. Yelling as loud as he could he cried, "Hallo ah sed!"

This made the men stop. "Whut hiz it, boy?" asked one of them.

"Heez daid," the boy responded.

"Hooz daid?"

173

"Editiah Jownes iz daid!"

"Who'n hail faihre iz Editiah Jownes?" asked an irritated man.

"Yew know him, he's the feller yur tearin this bildin aport fer. Yew know, the whun wawnts teh git beptaized."

The stunned men were utterly silent. Then one of them drawled, "Yew meen Jedidiah Jones?"

"Yih, yih, thet's thuh whun," the boy said. "Ah cudn' unnerstan the widder Murrideth tew good, she wuz bawlin', an' she wuz wailin' 'bout thuh cherch bein' torn tuh bitz fer nuthin', an' she wuz teuw fat tuh cum ep tchere hurseff tuh tell yew, sew she sint me."

One of the men volunteered to go to town and find out whether the boy knew what he was talking about. Sure enough, Jones died a day earlier. He was found in his apartment, and the landlord called the coroner, who called the mortician. Jones's already-stiff body was completely frozen from the rigor mortis that had set in, and the tangled ball of his corpse required a team of men to maneuver it through the door bit by bit, and roll it into the hearse.

The next morning, being church day, found the lock-jawed congregation sitting in stony silence in the scattered pews of the dismantled sanctuary. Everyone stared straight ahead, albeit at the oblique angles of the displaced pews, waiting for the service to end. When the altar call ended folks gathered outside, and could not help but talk about Jones.

"Thuh poor man," a woman said. "Ah am so sick about this."

"Itz lak thuh prichher said, thuh Lawrd werks in misteerius wayz. Sum'r mint tuh be sayved, n' sum eernt. We trahd, n' owr heerts wer n' thuh raht playce.

174

That iz all thuh Lawrd lewks fer."

CERN

Vanity of vanities, says the Preacher,
vanity of vanities! All is vanity.

Ecclesiastes 1:2 (ESV)

The great spokes of the primary magnet of the Large Hadron Collider formed a brilliant, multi-colored mandala behind the scientist standing at a lectern at its exact center. The lectern itself was sleek and modern and made of machined stainless steel; its microphone was so small as to be nearly invisible.

Dressed in a crisp khaki suit with razor-thin lapels, the short man favored a white shirt and a black string tie, the silver tips of which rested upon the top of his endomorph's belly. A thick tuft of straight black hair and a scrupulous Vandyke dyed jet-black completed the portrait of a self-assured man in his fifties.

"Good morning ladies and gentlemen," he began in a formal tone, "and welcome to this press conference of the Conseil Européen pour la Recherche Nucléaire. You will hear me call it CERN throughout the briefing."

"My name is François Kohelét, and I am the Director General here at CERN. I am so very pleased to announce that under my direction we have completed all preliminary testing protocols for the Large Hadron Collider, the LHC, and we at CERN are now prepared to uncover the secrets of the universe and usher in a new age of peace, wisdom, and prosperity."

The dozens of correspondents in the gallery shifted a bit, and someone coughed in the stagnant air.

"I apologize for the staleness of the air, but as you may imagine ventilation can at times be difficult in a facility so large yet so confined. Before I begin discussing this historic event, I think it necessary to spend a few moments reviewing the history of CERN, and the selfless contributions of the thousands who have worked so very hard to bring us to this moment." As he began to relax, Kohelét's voice began wheezing in a way that produced a slight whistle.

"You are precisely 300 meters below the surface of the Earth in an area we call SHEOL, the Super Hadron Energy Output Laboratory. We really don't live in any sort of regular time here, and do not know whether it is day or night. Time is, if you will, suspended here below the earth, which is fitting for the very important work we do because we will use the LHC housed in SHEOL to look backwards into time to the nanoseconds following the very birth of the cosmos. To do so, we will use a revolutionary process called Molecular Output Linear Energy Collision Habitation, or MOLECH for short.

"Please forgive me if I become too technical when speaking about CERN, but I am so passionate about this project that at times it absorbs me and I forget that I am not speaking to peers, but to lay persons. So I will do my very best to discuss the LHC in terms such that even a child might understand, since we want to be certain that your readers and viewers can understand how CERN is a monument, no a temple where science will shine as the bright beacon of truth for mankind.

"Ahem. CERN began as an idea among geniuses," he whistled, "and it stands today upon the shoulders of geniuses. Its fruit has already made itself evident, and is transforming mankind. Rubbia and van der Meer won the Nobel Prize for discovering weak gauge bosons here. A humble employee, Tim Berners-Lee, created the World Wide Web, HTML, and http so scientists could share their information and data. Little did he know that it would forever change mankind, and enable the Internet to become a technological miracle familiar to us all. I could go on, but time does not permit.

"As you saw during your travels here, CERN is at the foot of beautiful Mont Blanc, the highest in all of Europe, and the stunning Jura mountains can be seen in the distance. CERN is a celebration of diversity, and a truly international collaboration ministered by Europe, with countries such as Russia, Japan, Israel, Turkey, and the United States having observer status. It lies on the borders of France and Switzerland, so we have true international parity.

"Thousands of scientists work here. They have jointly constructed this monumental machine, with its glorious architecture, that must surely be called a crowning achievement of mankind. Together, we have created from nothing the CERN accelerators, and as the astronomers of old looked to the heavens to see God, we shall look inward to the heavens of the subatomic universe, and find absolute truth.

"I have on the screen before you a simple rendering of the accelerators. As you can see, there are three loops, including one small loop inside a larger one. We will start beams of protons out here, at the lower loop, and run them on parallel superconducting magnetic tracks through the first loop, where they will gather momentum to approximately eighty-seven (87) percent of the speed of light. They will then move on to the larger loop where they will separate onto opposing tracks at 99.999 percent of the speed of light. And then the protons will collide, at a rate of millions of times per second, and we shall see those majestic moments in the milliseconds that followed the Big Bang.

"There is a certain poetry, if you will, to the design of the LHC. There are, of course, the three loops, or circles. The circle is an ancient mystical symbol of the invariable total quantity of energy distributed throughout the universe, and, of course, we physicists deal with just that, the energy of the universe.

"And the number three is also an ancient religious symbol for the formula for the creation of the worlds. Now this is, of course, a coincidence, but it does have a certain elegance that should be appreciated. And some of us, in jest of course, refer to the loops as the Holy Trinity."

Kohelét's whistle now had a moderate canter. "Returning to our discussion of the LHC, everything in the Universe is made up of small particles, and these particles behave according to the laws of a few fundamental forces. Many particles are stable and form normal matter, but others live mere fractions of a second and decay into unstable particles.

"Is this not like life itself? All of these particles coexisted for the merest of instants after the Big Bang, and began their slow evolution into the cosmos as we know it. Only the greatness of a facility like CERN can resurrect the energy sufficient to bring these particles back to life. We will collide particles at speeds previously unreached by man, and by destroying, we will create. And in so doing, we will look back into time, and recreate those conditions present at the origin of the universe. We will view the creation as gods.

"I am certain that some of you will ask why it

is necessary to have a facility as unique as CERN. I anticipate you, and tell you that we need to understand the particle formation of the stars, the earth, the moon, the trees, and everything else. Yes, that includes us!" Kohelét's whistle began to turn dry. "We are nothing more than masses of particles assembled from the stuff of the universe, and that makes us the universe itself!"

"In doing so we will also understand reality itself, for we will be able to unlock the secrets of the nature of mass. How particles have any mass at all is a mystery that we intend to solve. As we all know, particles gain mass through the Higgs mechanism because matter particles and force carriers interact with the Higgs boson, and the strength of this reaction gives rise to mass. Now…. heh heh, forgive me, I see heads nodding, and I forget that I am not among colleagues.

"Perhaps this will pique your curiosity. We are looking for the God Particle, what physicists call the Higgs boson, and that is the real business of CERN. It is the Higgs boson that mediates the mass of particles and will give us the answer to many of the mysteries of the universe. There are unseen forces, strong and weak forces, forces that hold molecules together, and forces that tear them apart. We cannot see these forces, we cannot feel them, but we have faith that they exist. I boldly predict that we will find the Higgs boson, and then the Nobel Prizes will flow like champagne!

"Now, I think it is appropriate at this time to take questions from members of the press corps. You, sir, on the front row. You have a question?

"Yes, Barry Dingle, United Blogosphere. The readers on the Web want to know more about the energy generated by the LHC. The press kit indicates that the energy output is equivalent to eleven mosquitoes in motion."

"That's correct." Kohelét realized that his voice had become a whisper, so he sipped water from a plastic bottle.

"Isn't this an awful lot of trouble and expense for such a small output? I mean, it sounds to me like you could get that out of a flashlight battery."

"No, no, no," Kohelét said quickly. "You misunderstand. It is the energy output of eleven mosquitoes in one million millionth of the space a mosquito occupies."

"Well that's quite a trick. How do you guys get them so small?"

"Get what so small?"

"The mosquitoes."

"Sir, are you jesting?" asked Kohelét.

"No, if you're going to spend seven billion dollars shrinking mosquitoes I think that the public ought to know how you do it."

"What an asinine question!" croaked Kohelét. "I will move on to someone else. You, Madame."

"Thank you, Monsieur Kohelét. Stephanie Count with *The Economist*. The press kit states that the cost to date is seven billion Euros. What is the final cost?"

"Eleven billion Euros."

"A follow up, please. How many times has the cost estimate been revised?"

"Fifteen."

"And do you expect further revisions?"

"Yes. Science is not exact when it comes to cost, but we are confident that the final price will be under twenty billion Euros. And the benefits that man will reap cannot have a price fixed upon them."

"Thank you, sir."

"Yes, you, sir," Kohelét rasped.

"Thank you, Harry Animé from *Nature*. What practical applications may we expect to see from the work at CERN?"

"Thank you for the intelligent question. You may expect many. As mentioned, the World Wide Web was born here. We have also developed methods for faster computer data transmission, and medicine will benefit from the work here. Research in Hadron use, such as beams of protons, is used to direct specific streams of particles at tumors without harming surrounding tissue, so you may expect further advances in areas that will preserve precious human life from the ravages of cancer. And we have developed a thin film application here, called a getter, that captures stray particles. It will help with solar panels and those refrigerators the Americans treasure so much. And the discoveries here will even find their way into ordinary goods like hairdryers."

"And how is the public to know that CERN is a success?

"Sir," answered Kohelét, "the public is not our judge. Our judge is not God or governments, but nature. If we make a mistake, nature will not hesitate to punish us."

"A new questioner, please," Kohelét said. "You, sir."

"Thank you, John Masskop from the Theosoph News Network. Do you know Dr. Lisa Randall, the Harvard physicist?"

"Why yes I do, she is a brilliant colleague. She has performed valuable work here at CERN."

"I would like your reaction please to a quote of hers. 'We have no understanding of the Bang of the Big Bang. We understand many aspects of the universe's later evolution, but not how it began.' Would you agree?"

"That is beyond the scope of the work here at CERN…"

"Perhaps, but do you agree with Dr. Randall?"

"Yes, I do."

"So science has no understanding of the cause of the Big Bang, or even the cause of what preceded the Big Bang?"

"Well, no, but that really is outside the work we do here, so…"

"Wouldn't you consider this an important topic? If science asks questions about the natural world, then shouldn't we look for the true origin of the universe, and not spend billions looking for the milliseconds that follow its creation?"

"Perhaps we will go in that direction next, but what we are about here at CERN is…"

"Isn't CERN going about the problem backwards?"

"What do you mean?"

"CERN looks backward into time to find intermediate causes. Isn't it more logical to start at the very beginning, and build the foundation before you construct the house?"

"No, no, no, we use the pure logic of science, and the methods used here are those developed by the giants in our field."

"But there has to be a first cause, doesn't there? There is no creation from nothing without an unmoved mover, is there?"

"Sir," answered Kohelét, "you are trying to

185

interject religion into science, and science into religion." Kohelét's whistling was producing tiny bits of spittle that landed on the microphone. He hoped no one saw.

"I am simply following up on your earlier comment that God is not the judge of CERN. You said that nature is the judge. Aren't you trying to prove that God does not exist?"

"No, God must prove to us that he exists."

"Thank you for your candid answer."

Kohelét took a small puff from an inhaler he brought out of his pocket. "Forgive me, I am somewhat asthmatic, and the air down here sometimes grows quite rank. Time will permit only a few more questions. Sir?"

"John Blank with Postmodern Review. You stated that nature is the judge of whether CERN succeeds. Who is to judge whether nature has judged?"

"I am quite certain I do not follow you."

"Well Monsieur Kohelét, you have talked quite a lot about the Higgs boson, and it is fair for us to ask if the pursuit of Higgs will drive the results at CERN. How do we know that man, and not nature, judges the results at CERN?"

"Ridiculous."

"But what is success for one scientist may not be success for another, true?"

"No, not at all. That is utterly contrary to the scientific method."

"Many would not agree with you, Monsieur Director. Many believe that each has his own right to the truth, and that objective truth is impossible. You yourself have spoken of the quest for Higgs and how the Nobel prizes will flow like champagne. And, no doubt, so will your funding. Some would say that this is a quest by science to discover grants and prizes, and not some universal truth!"

"That is preposterous!" rasped Kohelét. "That is all, that is all," he said with a wave of his hand, "we are out of time."

****

The Large Hadron Collider was a stunning success. The first formal runs produced billions of collisions captured by the ATLAS detector. The world looked at pictures showing the spontaneous geometry of subatomic particles that exploded into straight lines, chains, and chaotic circles. As predicted, the Higgs Boson revealed itself, and early results confirmed the mathematical models of multiple dimensions.

The mood at CERN was elated. Ecstatic teams of scientists gorged themselves on the petabytes of data that streamed out. One scientist was especially intrigued with the renderings of the Higgs boson. He spent days looking at thousands of images; there was something about them that disturbed him, so he met with his supervisor to discuss his concerns.

"Jean," he said, "I cannot tell you why I believe this, but I am beginning to think that I am seeing letters in the images of the Higgs boson."

"What! You have been underground too long. Your brain is stale. You should go to the Alps and ski, take a woman with you. I'll approve the leave."

"No, no, it's nothing I am dreaming, I am certain that I can see the vaguest of letters, or writings, or something among the paths and the decays and the jets. I can't point to any single image or trace, but it's a sense I have."

"And what about this sense, what do you want me to do?"

"I need some resources from the Farm."

"The computer farm?"

"Yes. And I will need two or three people to help me with some programming to do image analysis."

"This is most unusual. I haven't heard anything about any letters or writings coming out of the LHC or ATLAS, but ah! This is CERN! We are all geniuses. Get your people and computers, and let me know when you come up with something."

A few weeks later the complaints began to stream in. The imaging team kept demanding more and more computer resources. The supervisor called the scientist in for an explanation.

"Heribert, I am told that you are demanding as much as twenty-five (25) percent of our computing power here. Do you know how much time you are pulling away from the other projects?"

"Yes, yes, I do Jean, but we are getting results! We are actually starting to identify some letters!"

"What! Do not tease me, Heribert, I am serious. The Director General himself called me this morning wanting to know what the hell is going on."

"We are slowly imaging letters from the Higgs boson. We have had the computers scan tens of thousands of them, and it isn't just me, everyone on the team sees them. We cannot stop talking about it. I swear! A message of some sort!"

"*Sacrebleu!* What do you mean you are seeing letters?"

"I mean letters from an alphabet. It looks like Greek, or Cyrillic, or something like that. No one I know here knows either of the languages, so it's a bit of a puzzle."

"Whom have you told about this?"

"No one. We agreed to keep it among ourselves so we don't get laughed out of CERN."

"No one is laughing. You have hundreds of computers tied up, and the Farm is so hot that the facility fire marshal is complaining. This cannot go on."

"You have to run interference for me on this one, Jean. We are close. I think that in two weeks I will have something to show. I promise. I am not making this up. There really is something out there."

"I will give you one week. I can stall the Director that long. One week, but no more. Now get the hell out of my office, Heribert."

The supervisor quickly forgot about Heribert. He was due to go on leave, and his mind drifted among food, and sex with his mistress, and ....

Brang! Brang! went the clipped ring of his telephone.

"Hello?"

"This is the Director General. Do you remember me?"

Ack! "Yes Monsieur Director, how may I help you?"

"I asked you over a week ago about the drain on computer usage by your unit, idiot. Did you forget about me?"

Had it been a week already? "No sir, of course not. I spoke with the scientist in charge of the use, and he had a very good explanation of his requirements."

"Such as?"

"He believes that he is finding letters of the Greek language or some other alphabet in the images of the

Higgs boson."

The voice gasped, and then whistled, "Ass! Tell me why I should not send the security team down to your office right now and have you thrown out."

Jean's stomach turned to stone, and he flatulated. "Because… because it is true. Heribert is finding letters in the images of the Higgs boson!"

"Swine! I am personally ordering you to shut down the team immediately! The computer usage has actually grown another eight percent since I called you. Get down there right now and shut it down, or you will be selling sausages from a cart outside the lavatory!"

But before Jean could get from behind his desk Heribert came through the door.

"We found it! We found it!"

"It's a damned good thing you did, imbecile! I was on my way to fire you. Good God, you look terrible. When was the last time you slept?"

"Not since you and I last met nine days ago."

"Nine days?" thought Jean. Where had the time gone?

"You have to see this," said Heribert. "We actually finished the analysis three days ago, and I've had no less than three other sets of physicists look at it! It's there! It's there!"

"What are you talking about, fool?"

"Hidden deep in all the Higgs boson data we found a sentence, you can't argue about the data, it's a sentence, and one of the techs recognized it as Greek, some ancient form of Greek, but no one here knows anything about Greek; but you can't argue about the data, it's all there, just as the others, so we're going to have to find someone who does know Greek, who can

190

tell us what this means, so I need for you to…"

"Shut up, idiot! Let me see what you are raving about." Jean looked, and could make no sense of the strange characters. A few of them he recognized from their use in physics equations, but the rest looked like gibberish.

"I'm not calling anyone until I can confirm this madness you're raving about. Sit down!"

After a few phone calls, a shaky Jean managed to sit down at his desk. *Mon Dieu!* This I cannot believe. I must call the Director General himself."

After three tries, Jean was able to correctly dial the Director's number. After pleading with the receptionist, the Director came on the line.

"Did you do what I ordered?"

"No sir, I…"

"Vous avez le cervau d'un sandwich au fromage! I am hanging up the phone and calling security."

"Sir you must listen to me, they found … they found a sentence buried in all of the Higgs boson data. None of us reads Greek, and we need to find someone to translate it for us."

"Debile!," screamed the Director. "There are seventeen hundred brilliant scientists here, and you are telling me we need a professor of Greek! I am at this very moment calling security to have you arrested! You and the other madmen who commit sacrilege to the Higgs boson with your preposterous claims about secret letters in the Higgs boson; I will have you all arrested!"

"Monsieur Director, please, please, I have seen it myself, my very own eyes, three separate CERN teams have verified the analysis, I beg you, I beg your mother, please permit me to show this to you so you can see for yourself, so someone with your erudition and wisdom can judge the truth of this matter...."

"I will permit you and Heribert to come to my office solely to exercise my prerogative to personally dismiss the both of you from CERN and make certain that you cannot find employment doing so much as writing textbooks. Present yourself immediately!"

By the time the disheartened Jean and Heribert reached his office Kohelét had assumed an official demeanor. "Gentlemen, please come in. While you were coming I spoke with the chief counsel, who reminded me that there are certain protocols that must be observed prior to dismissal. Accordingly, I must examine this "writing" that you have made such extraordinary claims about. I presume that you will forgo the presence of a stenographer, which, of course, you have the right to?"

"Yes, yes, of course," they both said.

"Very well. Let me see the document." Kohelét examined it briefly and said, "I can make nothing of this gibberish. You seem to be correct that this is Greek, but how do I know that this is not some sort of a joke?"

"Please Monsieur," said Heribert, "my team has worked like dogs. We have forsaken food, our families, bathing, we have commanded large amounts of computer time...."

"I am well aware of that. It was reported to me this morning that there was a small fire at the Farm four days ago."

"Yes sir. We did what was required. It became apparent to us that qualitative analysis was yielding data that translated itself into the letters of the Greek alphabet. We knew that we were taxing the computers, but we knew, we sensed that the Higgs boson had some secret."

"You sensed?" said the Director. "Sir, we are scientists, not fortune tellers."

"It wasn't just me, sir, we had eight people working on this around the clock. We ignored everything but the Higgs boson renderings. Then we had three other qualitative analysis teams reviews verify the results. This is no joke."

"Indeed. I am also informed that protocols require me to proceed to the next step, since you insist that you are acting properly. I am required to refer the matter to a neutral to accept or reject your assertions. Since I know of no one who has any expertise, I am open to your suggestions."

"Well sir," said Heribert, "I was for a time a student of religion at the Sorbonne. I remember a respected professor of ancient languages, Haäckmunney, a Jew. I never studied under him, and he is probably retired by now, but I am certain that he can be located for consultation."

"I will make the arrangements, and will contact you when we are ready to proceed. Do not leave CERN, and discuss this with no one," Kohelét said.

The very next morning the two men reported to the Director's private conference room. A technician had prepared for a video conference, and the heads of various departments were present.

"Gentlemen, please be seated. We are ready to begin. I am now starting the video record of this proceeding in accordance with section ten point twenty-three, sub-paragraph eight, sub- sub-section 'a' of the CERN protocols manual for the dismission of employees."

After reciting the presence of the department heads for qualitative and quantitative analysis and the CERN lawyer, Kohelét instructed the technician to establish a video connection with the Sorbonne. A face suddenly appeared.

"Good morning, Professor, this is François Kohelét, Director General of CERN. We are here this morning to obtain your expert and unbiased reading of a script that has been derived through the analysis of certain quantitative data from the Large Hadron Collider here at CERN. Are you ready to proceed?"

"Why yes, and good morning to you, Director, and all others," said Haäckmunney, whose massive head filled the screen. His large nose was pitted, and his grizzled hair and beard were splayed in every direction such that a greyish halo seemed to encircle his head. He wore tiny spectacles and his skin was permanently flushed. The smoke from the pipe sticking out of the side of his mouth seemed to be trapped in his hair and beard, giving the appearance that his head was floating in a cloud.

"Very well. I will now display the text in question."

Kohelét pressed a button, and the screen flashed the script:

οὐκ ἔστιν πᾶν πρόσφατον ὑπὸ τὸν ἥλιον

"Professor Haäckmunney," Kohelét continued, "Do you see the text?"

"Yes I do."

"Does it mean anything to you?"

Haäckmunney cackled as he pulled his pipe away from his mouth. His head shook as he laughed, loosing the smoke from his beard and hair, which drifted up and out of view.

"Why yes, I do recognize this, it is very familiar

194

to me. It is from the Septuagint, which is the Greek translation of the Hebrew Bible. It looks to be verbatim."

"Are you quite certain, Professor?"

"Oh yes, there is no doubt about it. Allow me to pull my copy of the Septuagint for verification. Yes, here it is, in fact, this is verbatim from Ecclesiastes."

Haäckmunney read the Greek aloud. "And you say you found this embedded in some of your physics data?"

"That is the claim, yes," answered Kohelét.

"This is fascinating in the extreme," Haäckmunney said. "Perhaps I could come there soon and see how you came about this information. We do not often see the divine appear so clearly in nature."

"Yes, yes, perhaps, but we need to know now. What does it mean?"

"It is translated as, 'there is nothing new under the sun.'"

"What? Could you please repeat that?"

"It means, 'there is nothing new under the sun.' I'll read the verse in Ecclesiastes it goes with:

What has been is what will be,

and what has been done is what will be done,

and there is nothing new under the sun.

"Does that mean anything to you?" asked the Professor.

A long silence followed.

"Hello, CERN, are you still there?"

Someone shouted, "Check the computers!"

The lawyer gasped, "Is this some sort of a joke?"

The head of quantitative analysis yelped, "It is a coincidence!"

Kohelét was the last to speak. He whistled, "This is apostasy!"

www.ingramcontent.com/pod-product-compliance
Lightning Source LLC
Chambersburg PA
CBHW031431250626
47155CB00004B/1702